Legend

(Lochaidh)

(Book Two)

by

Terri Reid

Eochaidh – Legend of the Horsemen (Book Two)

by Terri Reid

Copyright © 2018 by Terri Reid

The author would like to thank all those who have contributed to the creation of this book: Richard Reid, Sarah Reid, Camille McDaris, Peggy Hannah, Mickey Claus, Terrie Snyder, Maureen McDermott Marella, and Hillary Morgan Gadd.

And especially to the wonderful readers who are starting this whole new adventure with me. Thank you all!

Eochaidh (Yeo-hay) of <u>Celtic</u> origin, meaning horseman.

Chapter One

King Arthur's Court

The age of Arthur was nearing its end. A shadow had crept over the land of Camelot, a specter of the sins of mankind. Trust had been replaced with betrayal, honor with duplicity, and love with envy. The Knights of the Round Table had been torn between fealty and compassion. Choose the king or choose the lady and the knight? There were no winners in either choice.

The king sat alone in the chamber of the great Round Table, his shoulders bent, his head in his hands, burdened by the knowledge of his mistakes, his human frailty. The gray stone walls that had once echoed with laughter and camaraderie now sat as a silent tomb, surrounding the once and future king. The round table which had once gleamed with polish and pride was now scarred and split, the remnants of the last great battle. The banners that had proudly displayed the colors of the knights, his beloved knights, were torn and tattered.

Arthur lifted blood-stained eyes to the sky and whispered, "Has it all been for naught? Is there nothing to be gained?"

He lowered his head once more and sat in the deathly silence of his living tomb.

His solemn meditation was interrupted by the sound of footsteps coming toward the chamber. Instinctively, his body was alert and awaiting a fight. He reached for the sword no longer at his side and sighed. "Why do I even fight?" he whispered. "I should welcome an end to this pained existence."

The giant door was pushed open. Arthur turned slowly, anticipating the worst. But the visitor was no foe. Arthur looked at the fledgling knight— Tristan of Lochtyn—the youngest of those who had served at the Round Table. At only twenty-three years, his body was strong and honed as the warrior he was. His chestnut hair fell forward onto his forehead. His dark brown eyes, which had often sought Arthur's for direction and confirmation, now held concern and confusion. Tristan had always looked to Arthur for guidance, and Arthur felt another stab of pain as he knew he had betrayed the young man's trust. Tristan's face, which had been eager and fearless, now was weary and hesitant.

He has aged, Arthur thought bitterly, *and I stole his years.*

"What would you have of me, Tristan of Lochtyn?" Arthur asked sadly.

Tristan slowly approached the table. He too saw change. His beloved king was no longer a demigod, but a man. His blonde hair had grayed, his blue eyes dimmed, and his proud shoulders stooped. He was a man fraught with regrets—a man burdened with sorrow. *But,* the young knight reminded himself, *he is still my king, still my leader.*

Many of the knights had left the land of legend, seeking their own adventures, but a loyal few stayed, loyal to their king, loyal to the land and people of Camelot. But more than that, they were loyal to the oath of the Order of Chivalry of Arthur's court, the oath they took to protect the distressed, maintain the right, and live a stainless existence.

"Your majesty," he began, kneeling before his king.

The king shook his head. "Do not kneel before me, lad."

Tristan hesitated, stood and then began to speak. "I have learned of a plot…"

Arthur waved his hand to halt his words. "I want no more of plots or intrigue," he said wearily. "I want peace."

Tristan shook his head, confused. "But your majesty, Morganna…"

The king dropped his head into his hands. "I will not hear that name spoken in this castle," he said, his voice angry and pointed.

"I understand, your Majesty..."

The king's bitter laugh cut off his words. "Do you?" he asked, looking up and meeting Tristan's eyes. "Do you think you understand, young Tristan? I think not."

The king lowered his head again. "I can no longer act as your king," he said, so softly that Tristan had to lean forward to hear the words. "I can no longer trust my decisions. I am afraid that I am very much a coward."

Arthur shook his head sadly, and Tristan felt a fist of fear clench in his stomach. "Perhaps I always was a coward."

He waved his arm, dismissing Tristan. "Go. Take your plot to Merlin. Perhaps he will be of some use to you."

Tristan moved toward the king, his arm outstretched, his king's pain mirrored in his eyes.

"My king…" he whispered.

Arthur once again rested his head in his hands. "Go away," the king sighed sadly, "just go away."

Tristan backed slowly out of the room, his eyes never leaving the sight of his king, his exemplar, bowed in abject misery. The dark shadow creeping through the midst of Camelot seemed to encompass his heart. If the king could be defeated, then what hope was there for the rest of them? What hope for Camelot?

Stumbling from the castle, he stopped at the open door and gazed around at the courtyard. The scene before him reflected the attitude of the king.

The villagers slogged through ankle-deep mud, their faces somber and despondent. Children huddled in corners, afraid to laugh and play. The infirm no longer begged for alms but turned their heads away from the street and readied themselves for death.

The sides of the castle were marked with the visible damages of the war, blackened stones and destroyed battlements, but the scars of the people were deeper and invisible except to those who took the time to see. Hope and promise were gone. Only despair and fear filled their hearts.

The young knight's resolve wavered. How could he protect the people from misery? How could he give back to them what had been ruthlessly taken away? How could he, a mere knight, defend them from an even more desperate future? For a moment, his heart trembled with fear. He should run away! He should leave Camelot! He should forget about contacting Merlin.

He stopped suddenly, examining his thoughts. These weren't his words; these weren't his feelings. What was happening?

Black magic! He felt the darkness once again try to touch the corner of his mind, once again try to keep him from his task. Pushing it away, he dashed across the courtyard to the stables.

The stables were a skeletal ruin of what they used to be, but they still offered some protection. Entering, he saw his dappled gray Iberian stallion tied to a post, waiting patiently for his master. He untied the reins and quickly mounted the massive horse, before the fog of black magic could assail his thoughts again.

"To Merlin," he whispered to his mount. "For Camelot."

Chapter Two

Morganna scowled with displeasure as she stared into her scrying bowl, watching the young knight gallop out of the courtyard. She'd touched his thoughts, she knew she had. For a moment, he'd allowed the darkness to creep in and conquer him. But then he pushed it aside and regained hope. There was something about this young knight, Tristan of Lochtyn, that concerned her. Hope was not an emotion she wanted spreading throughout Camelot. Despair made the people more malleable, so much easier to enslave.

She watched him take the road towards the woods and laughed softly.

Merlin. The fool was taking his concerns to Merlin.

"You will find nothing there but a broken, old mage, wrapped up in his own regrets and guilt," she said to the image in the water. "He will not be able to defeat me. He is far too weak."

She studied the woods as the young knight cantered toward the entrance. The woods were old, and the magic within was even older. She thought about sending some of her men out to intercept him. Young Tristan wouldn't even get a chance to meet with Merlin. A knife or sword through his heart would certainly stop him if her magic couldn't.

But she bent over the scrying bowl and studied the young man's face. It was a noble face, with determination and courage in his eyes. She shook her head. "No, such an honorable creature would have followers who would find it necessary to avenge his death," she said sadly. "And that would become so tedious. There must be a way to stop him and send a message that I will not be trifled with."

She stepped away from the bowl and walked across the stone floor of her tower chamber and stopped in the doorway. She reached up and pulled down on a long, braided rope just outside the room. Moments later, one of her henchmen appeared and immediately, upon seeing her, bowed abjectly. "Milady," he said, cowering slightly. "What would you have me do?"

"I would like you to discover who the associates of the young knight Tristan of Lochtyn are," she said. "Then discover what weaknesses they have or secrets they hold, so we can use them to our advantage."

"Aye, milady," the henchman immediately replied. He turned and ran down the steep, stone stairs towards the main entrance to the castle, calling for his fellow conspirators as he ran.

Morganna smiled with satisfaction and walked back to the bowl on her stand. The young knight was hesitating at the forest's edge. Perhaps he could feel the power of the old magic. She placed her hand over the bloodstone amulet she wore and rubbed her thumb over its cold exterior until she could feel it vibrate in response to her touch. "Well, my young Tristan," she whispered, "you are aware of the magic around you. Not many knights are that astute." She sighed sadly. "It's too bad you will be dead before the week's end. You had such a promising future."

Chapter Three

Merlin's tower was not within Camelot, but miles away on a hill at the edge of the forest. Tristan had heard that Merlin not only preferred his privacy but also preferred to look down on the occupants of Camelot, rather than associate with them. Galloping through the farm fields just before the forest, he glanced up to the sky and saw the stone tower in the distance, its highest point nearly touching the clouds.

A faint shudder crept across his heart. He had heard many had perished at the hands of Merlin, and he wondered if he would return alive. His horse sensed his trepidation and shied away from the opening of the woods. "Now there," he said softly, patting his steed on the side of his neck. "Don't pay any attention to me. Just the wanderings of an over-active imagination. I'm sure Merlin is a fine fellow."

His mount snorted, whether in agreement or disbelief Tristan could never tell, but then galloped forward and entered the forest. The soft loam hushed the stallion's hooves, and the noise of the woods echoed all around them.

Tristan straightened in the saddle, his sword at the ready, prepared for attack by whatever magic dwelt within these borders.

The wind whistled through the trees, whispering the warnings of those who had dared travel this path before. The trees bent together, forming a canopy of green like a spider's web, enticing the prey to come closer and deeper into the trap. The creatures of the woods skittered in the underbrush and across the tree tops, watching the man and horse and warning those who would need to know.

After traveling for several miles, the path opened into a small glen, and in the center was a sparkling blue lake, pristine and inviting. Tristan guided his horse to the shore and dismounted. "We'll stop for a moment," he said, patting his horse's neck. "You drink while I gather my wits."

The horse stepped cautiously forward, stopping several inches from the water, and leaned forward to drink. "Frightened of sea monsters?" Tristan teased. "I assure you, nothing so fearsome lives within the confines of this body of water."

Suddenly, the light began to change, as if a cloud had moved away from the sun. The air was crisper, and a soft mist began to form on the top of the water. He stepped back and grabbed hold of the saddle's pommel, ready to mount up and escape. But something, some inner voice, held him in place, and he released the saddle and slowly walked back toward the lake.

Stepping forward, his hand on the reins to calm his horse, he waited at the water's edge. "Is this some trickery?" he asked. "Is this, Master Merlin, a test of some kind?"

The mist on the water began to foam, a surging of power from beneath. His horse snorted and pranced in fear. Tristan tightened his hold on the reins but kept his eyes on the lake.

The water bubbled, as if the lake now boiled with heat. Suddenly a woman came up from the depths of the lake. She had long, blonde hair, and her body was draped in a royal blue robe. Her face was beyond mortal beauty, and looking at her, he felt hope burn once again in his heart. He knew her, at least he knew of her. He fell to his knee. "My lady," he said, bowing his head.

She smiled at Tristan. "You may rise, Sir Tristan."

He stood at her request.

"You have seen Arthur?" she asked.

He nodded. "I have seen the king, but he is not the man I have known," he admitted. "There is a shadow of darkness and despair in the hearts of all who reside in Camelot—not only the king, but the entire population. Camelot is dead, my lady."

"Camelot is not dead, young knight," she whispered. "Only lying in wait, like a rose in the winter to bloom once again in its season. Your king may once again rule as he was meant to rule."

His heart leapt with hope, but it was hard to believe her words. "I do not want to doubt you," he said. "But how can there be hope?"

"You, young knight, hold the fate and the hope of Camelot in your hands," she continued, her voice echoing inside Tristan's mind. "Follow your heart, to wherever it leads, and you will save Camelot. You will save us all."

The wind once again began to whisper through the forest. Tristan stepped forward, toward the lady as she began to descend into the lake.

"Wait," he called. "Will you tell me no more?"

"Follow your heart," was the answer that echoed once again in his mind.

Chapter Four

The tower Merlin inhabited was at the other
end of the forest. After his encounter with the Lady
of the Lake, Tristan gave his horse its head, and they
galloped at full speed the rest of the way. The forest
stopped several yards before the tower, as if some
magic kept the vegetation from moving any farther.

The hill on which the tower perched was
more covered in stone and thistles than grass and
trees. No vegetation grew up the sides of the round
tower. Its massive, gray boulders stood cold and
foreboding on the top of the hill. Tristan studied the
stronghold. It was unlike any building he'd ever seen.
Large blocks of limestone teetered on other blocks,
ascending into the air. There seemed to be no mortar
holding the massive stones in place and no logical
explanation as to why they still all remained in place.
They were truly a hodgepodge of giant stones
tumbled together to create a dwelling.

Tristan looked up and felt his stomach turn.
He had always felt queasy when he had to deal with
heights. Long ago he had decided he was a man

made for the earth, not the skies. Dismounting, he led his horse along the side of the hill to a cobblestoned pathway. He stopped when he reached the two large oak trees standing stark and bare at the start of the path to Merlin's lair. Before the shadows had come to Camelot, he had heard that Merlin's trees had always been lush and full, no matter the season. Another sign of the times.

He tied his mount loosely to a lower branch of the tree. "If I do not return," he whispered in his horse's ear, "pull yourself free and return to the stables."

The horse snorted and rubbed his massive head against the knight's chest. Tristan patted the horse's neck affectionately and then turned to face his task.

The pathway led to the front of the tower and a large oak door that was covered with symbols and runes. Tristan knew the signs had something to do with protection and prayed they did not turn intruders into frogs or lizards. Merlin did not have a reputation of having patience or understanding, quite the opposite. His repute was more of a dangerous and hot-tempered wizard with a foul disposition since the fall of Camelot.

Tristan's heart was thumping in his chest as he lifted his hand to the door. Even with the encouragement of the Lady of the Lake, he was unsure of his welcome. He laid his hand on the door, took a deep breath and pushed.

The hinges groaned and creaked, but the door opened wide enough for him to slip inside. In front of him was a tall, narrow, spiraling stone staircase that rather than hugging the walls traveled up the center of the tower to nearly fifty feet above his head. There were no railings on either side of the steps, and it seemed to Tristan that the entire structure was suspended in midair. Tristan walked around the edifice, trying to discern which laws of nature allowed the stairs to remain standing.

"The laws of nature are only used when absolutely necessary," a deep voice called from the heights. "If you wish to speak with me you must venture up."

Tristan swallowed and felt his body respond to his terror of heights as beads of sweat gathered on his forehead and his palms became moist. His stomach began to twist as he placed his first foot on the step. He stopped and took another deep breath. He was not a child, he scolded himself. He was a knight of the Round Table, and he had no time for infantile fears.

With a determined set to his jaw, he jogged quickly up the steps, keeping his eyes to the door at the top of the stairs. When he had traversed about thirty-five feet, the steps began to sway, rocking in an uneven circular motion. He was thrown off balance and fell to his knees.

Grabbing the edges of the stairs on either side, he felt his stomach heave as he glanced to the stone floor below him. He took a deep breath to calm his stomach and another one to calm his heart. Try as he might, the staircase's movement wouldn't allow him to stand, so he began the slow and painful process of crawling up the staircase to the top.

Sharp stone edges cut his hands and bruised his knees, but he continued. The staircase swayed back and forth, quickly increasing its momentum.

Finally, it was rotating in a full circle, and the doorway Tristan sought circled before his eyes.

He closed his eyes for a moment, but that made the sensation even worse. He opened them quickly. Sweat dripped down his forehead as he continued to climb, now keeping his focus on the rock and stone of the stair in front of him. He was sure he had traveled at least another twenty feet and glanced up, realizing with dismay that there was at least another twenty feet of climbing ahead of him.

He looked to the side. The tower was narrower towards the top, and the stairs barely slipped past without scraping against the walls. Tall, tapered windows flew by, and he could glimpse out and see far beyond the lands of Camelot.

As he turned back to his task, he heard noises coming from above him. A voice cried out in pain. "No, no, you will not take my powers, Morganna. I will die first."

"Merlin!" Tristan cried. He leapt to his feet, heedless of the rotation, and charged up the remaining stairs, his sword braced for a fight. Pausing at the very top, he waited just a moment, balancing on the balls of his feet until the staircase spun in front of the door, and then he leapt forward, ready to fight.

Tristan looked around the room, his sword at the ready. At first glance the room seemed to be empty. But he knew his ears had not deceived him. He moved forward slowly into the strange chamber. The top of the tower was still thirty feet above the floor of the chamber, and large windows in the roof filled the tower with light. Strange automations hung from the ceiling, reflecting light and spinning slowly, intertwining with each other.

The first floor was filled with tables that held all types of strange and unusual mechanisms. The table to the left of him held an ivory mortar and pestle with dried herbs scattered around it. Another table, farther away, held a metal cylinder from which fire escaped and heated a clear container filled with liquid. And still another table held strange boxes with the appearance of smooth, black stone.

A second story loft circled the chamber with shelves of books lining the round walls. There were numerous ladders on wheels that offered access from the loft to the first floor.

Tristan turned slowly, the hairs on the back of his neck warning him that things were not as they seemed. He lifted his sword to shoulder height, both hands gripping the hilt, ready to fight.

A movement in the far corner of the room caught his eye. The corner was covered and dark, but he sensed someone, or something, was hiding within. Lunging forward, he ran towards the corner, his sword poised to strike. Suddenly, the corner was filled with light so intense Tristan was momentarily blinded. He stumbled forward and slammed into a solid wall. Confused, because there was no wall in his proximity, he jumped back, the bright light no longer blinding his sight, and looked around to see that he was still in the middle of the room.

"What is this sorcery?" he called out.

The soft chuckle had Tristan turning quickly, but the slight, old man walking towards him had him lowering his sword to his side.

"Merlin?" he asked, astonished.

The old man with long, white hair and a flowing beard nodded benevolently, his long, thin pipe clenched between his teeth.

"Well done, my boy," Merlin said, walking slowly toward Tristan.

"You cried out for help," Tristan answered, sword still clenched in hand.

"I did indeed," Merlin replied. "And you responded immediately."

Tristan shook his head. "I don't understand. Where is the danger?"

Merlin smiled. "Come back with me to the door of my chamber," he said.

Merlin stood next to the doorframe and motioned for Tristan to look out onto the staircase. Tristan's body clenched as he looked down the narrow tower to the floor below. Unconsciously, he tightened his hold on the doorframe.

"You have a fear of heights?" Merlin asked.

Embarrassed, Tristan replied, "Yes, I am a flawed knight of the Round Table."

"Bah," Merlin replied impatiently. "You were afraid—and yet, you are here. Why is that?"

"I had to come," Tristan replied, confused. "I had to see you."

"You could have refused, you could have sent another."

"No," Tristan said forcefully. "There was no other. It had to be me."

"Ah," Merlin nodded. "And when you ascended my, er, staircase, was it easy?"

Tristan shrugged and turned away. "I...I had some trouble."

Merlin nodded, running his fingers down the length of his beard. "Ah, trouble, good, good," he said. "What kind of trouble?"

Tristan closed his eyes, lowered his head and sighed. "I had to crawl like a babe."

Merlin nodded. "Yet when you entered my chamber, you were not crawling. As I remember, you were more bounding into this room."

Tristan sighed and responded. "I heard you cry out..."

24

Merlin smiled and placed his hand on Tristan's shoulder. "Yes, you heard me cry out. And so, the concern you had for me overruled the fear you had of heights," Merlin said, turning Tristan to face him. "That, my young knight, is the truest form of courage."

Tristan shook his head. "No, Master Merlin, that is the duty of a knight."

Merlin chuckled. "So it is. So it is," he said. "Now, what brings you here, to Merlin's lair?"

Chapter Five

The air stank of stale ale and unwashed bodies. The newest patrons of the Rose and Crown Pub were a coarse and menacing collection, drawn like vultures to the dying corpse of Camelot. Tristan sat at a long, roughhewn table at the back of the large public room. His face was shielded by the hood of his dark, woolen cloak, which also hid the garments that proclaimed him a knight of the Round Table. He watched the door and sipped the tankard of ale before him.

As the door opened, cold, damp air and a large, red-headed giant of a man entered the room. His red beard and mustache were frosted from the cold, and the thick eyebrows over his green eyes were lowered in concentration. He gazed around the room slowly, dismissing all until his eyes met Tristan's. With more grace than one would think possible from such a large man, he moved through the room to Tristan's table.

"May I sit?" he asked.

Tristan nodded and signaled for another tankard.

The serving maid brought the overflowing tankard and set it in front of the large man. He picked it up, took a long, satisfying drink, then placed it back on the table with a thump and wiped his mouth with the back of his arm.

"Well, I'm here," he said. "What would you have me do?"

Tristan's eyebrows rose slightly. "What, Rufus, no questions? No demands for explanations?" Tristan asked.

The red-haired man smiled and took another gulp. "If I hadn't trusted you in the first place, laddie, I wouldn't be here now," he simply replied.

Tristan smiled and leaned across the table, grasping Rufus's large arm. "You're a good man, Sir Rufus, and I'm grateful you're my friend."

Rufus placed his large paw over Tristan's hand and looked into his eyes.

"Just make sure that this is worth leaving the warm arms of my own Fiona, and we'll stay friends."

Tristan laughed, and Rufus released his hand. "You are a true friend indeed to leave Fiona," Tristan said. "How is she?"

Rufus smiled, his eyes misting a little as he thought about his wife. "Ah, she's like the heather in the morning, as the dew softly rises to the sun," he sighed. "She is bonnie, so bonnie."

"And the little ones?" Tristan asked.

Rufus grinned. "Ach, they're filled with spit and vinegar, they are," he chuckled. "I thought girls were supposed to be prim and proper. These two are but two young lion cubs. Fiona will have quite a time making ladies out of them."

Tristan laughed. "As I recall, it was that very spirit that drew your eye to Fiona in the first place."

Rufus nodded. "Aye, laddie, watch out for the fiery ones. They'll lead you on a merry chase for the rest of your life." He sighed and finished off the rest of the tankard. "But it'll be a life worth living."

The door opened once again, and three men entered together. They were an odd combination—

one was slight and bespectacled, one tall and dark with a dangerous air, and the third an eager youth.

The youngest saw Tristan first, and his face alit with joy.

"Tristan, Tristan, here we are!" he called across the room.

Rufus rolled his eyes. "Andrew has the discretion of a pup."

Tristan nodded, trying to hide his grin. "Aye, but the heart of a lion."

Rufus chuckled.

The three men moved slowly, the eyes of many of the other patrons following them as they made their way across the room. The tall man of the group paused in the middle of the room and turned, staring back at those interested men. His black hair was shoulder length, his face lean and hard, and his eyes were grey and cold. He moved with the grace of a panther.

He slowly lifted his arms and drew his cloak back. A black eagle in flight graced the front of his doublet. A hush came over the room, and the eyes that had been so bold just moments before were now hidden and cautious.

"He killed his sister, you know. I heard he was in league with the dark forces."

The maid's voice was unnaturally loud in the hushed room. The tall man's head snapped toward the sound, and he held the frightened maid's gaze for a moment. The silly maid's face was ashen with fear. He held her gaze for a moment longer and then continued to the table to join Tristan and the others.

"Well, there goes the service for the evening," Rufus growled as the other men joined them. "You couldn't have been a little more discreet, Sir Garrett?"

Garrett's laugh was bitter and mocking. "Oh, discreet," he said, pulling off his gloves and laying them on the table. "Like our young friend Andrew here?"

At only eighteen, Andrew was the fledgling of the group. His face still held the fullness of youth, with the promise of hardness in a few years. Like a young Adonis, his curly, blonde hair and bright blue eyes drew the ladies to him like bees to a honey pot.

But Garrett's comment turned his eager smile into a look of shame. His face grew red, and he hung his head. "If only I had thought before I spoke…" he began.

"It would have been the first time," Garrett finished. "And it would have been a miracle."

"Leave the boy be," Tristan said. "His greeting did us no harm. They were suspicious before you entered the room."

He turned to the scholarly man seated next to him. "Duncan," he asked. "Were you able to decipher any of the notes I gave you?"

Duncan was the slightest built of the men at the table and the shortest. His shoulder-length light brown hair was drawn back and held in place by a leather thong so that the thinning on the top of his head was more visible. He had the look of a scholar, with round glasses perched on his nose and deliberate, exacting mannerisms in his actions. However, unbeknownst to most that saw him, he was a skilled warrior, and beneath the drab grey cloak was the body of a man who could fight if need be.

Duncan pulled an oilskin pouch out from underneath his cloak. He removed his rounded spectacles from his eyes and rubbed them with a white linen handkerchief before replacing them and opening the pouch.

The scroll he withdrew was aged and fragile. Duncan handled it with care. He pulled out a scrap of leather from farther down in the pouch and smoothed it across the table. Then he placed the scroll on the leather and rolled it open.

"These markings," he said as he pointed to some lines at the top of the scroll, "symbolize time. The arrows point both to the right and to the left."

"Does that mean direction?" Garrett asked.

"Aye, that's right," Duncan said, "but not direction as in North, South, East and West."

"What other direction is there?" asked Rufus. "Up and down?"

Duncan shook his head and lifted his eyes, meeting the gaze of each man before he continued. "No, there is past and present."

Tristan nodded. "That's what I had heard," he agreed. "That somehow she had a way to move between places in time."

Andrew shook his head. "But then she could go back before the king was born and kill his mother."

Duncan nodded at the young man. "An astute observance," he said. "But I believe that she can't go back further than her birth. She can only travel forward and return."

"How can that harm Camelot?" Andrew asked. "Who cares if she goes into the future? Good riddance to her."

Rufus shook his head. "With her power and her madness, she could create all kinds of mischief," he said. "She's not safe anywhere."

There was a moment of silence, and then Tristan spoke softly. "I saw the Lady of the Lake."

"You did what?" Garrett asked, astonished.

"I was on my way to Merlin, to tell him of my discovery," he said. "I stopped at the lake, and she appeared. She told me that Camelot was not destroyed, that it was just sleeping—like a rose in winter. She told me that whether it woke again was up to us."

"If she can go into the future, she can destroy Camelot again," Garrett said.

"If she can go into the future, she can destroy all we love," Rufus added.

Duncan rolled up the scroll and placed it back into the pouch.

"What would you have us do, Tristan?" he asked.

Tristan took a deep breath. "I would have us destroy the spell that gives her this power," he said.

"Meaning we must go to her castle." Garrett said, sitting back in his chair. "She is rarely gone from her castle. It sits on a lone inlet, with only one escape. It is guarded by dark magic. The odds of success are small. You ask us to risk our lives to attempt this foolish venture?"

Tristan looked at Garrett—brown eyes meeting grey ones.

"I do," he replied, laying his hand on the table.

Garrett sat forward on his chair and placed his hand on Tristan's.

"At your command, Tristan."

"And I," said Rufus, placing his hand on the other two.

"And I," said Andrew, joining the others.

Duncan shook his head and smiled.

"Well, someone with more brain than muscle ought to be there," he said, placing his hand on top of them all. "I am yours to command."

Tristan smiled at them, his eyes moist with emotion.

"We will defeat her," he said firmly.

"Aye," said Rufus. "We must."

Chapter Six

Rain cascaded against the cobblestone path that led to the stables alongside the inn. The shale stone was slippery, and Sir Andrew had to balance himself carefully as he hurried toward his assignation. He lifted his lantern a little higher to determine the pathway from the muddy earth surrounding it. It would not do to step into one of the brown-green puddles and have his polished boots smell of horse.

Finally, at the stables, he opened the door and slipped inside. The scent of sweet hay and manure assailed his nose immediately. But a sweeter, more subtle scent had him immediately turning around and stepping toward the shadows near the first stall.

"Anwyn," he whispered, stepping towards the lady in the shadows.

"Dowse your light so we are not discovered," she entreated, her words breathy and eager.

Nearly dropping the lantern on the straw floor, Andrew quickly turned and extinguished the light, plunging them both into darkness. He moved forward unsteadily. "Anwyn?"

"You came," she whispered, moving into his embrace. "I was so afraid you would forget about me."

His young heart pounded with excitement and desire. "Of course I came," he replied, trying to moderate his tone so he didn't sound too eager. "Anwyn, you are everything to me."

He swallowed nervously as he felt her hands slowly slide up his chest and her lips brush his jaw. "Anwyn?" he questioned tentatively, wrapping his arms around her waist and pulling her against him.

"Oh, Andrew," she gasped, her sweet breath caressing his cheek. "I've waited so long to have you hold me like this."

"You have?" he asked, his voice escaping his dry mouth in a squeak. He fumbled clumsily to pull her even closer and nearly knocked them both to the floor. But providence had them stumbling so she was pressed against the stable wall and he was tight against her. His movements were graceless as he pulled at the back of her dress, trying to untie her apron. "Oh, Anwyn," he wheezed, his ale-tainted breath assailing her nose. "I've dreamt of this with you. Dreamt of it so many times."

He finally untied the apron and moved his hands forward over her hips.

Quickly placing her hands over his so he couldn't proceed, she sighed loudly. "I've dreamt of it too, my dearest Andrew," she reached up and ran her tongue along his jawbone.

He gasped loudly, longing searing his body. "Yes," he breathed, struggling to pull his hands out from under hers and explore her curves more fully.

"But I cannot," she said pointedly. "I am promised to another."

Like a bucket of cold water, her words smothered the fire burning in his chest. "What?" he cried, shaking his head in disbelief. "No. You can't be. We were... I was..."

She lifted her delicate hand to his lips. "Shhhh," she pleaded. "I was only told this evening. My father was offered a settlement he could not refuse."

"But I spoke with your father," he argued. "I was going to bring him the settlement in a fortnight."

She laid her head against his chest and wept delicately. "I pleaded with my father," she sobbed. "I told him I would love no other but you."

"Yet, he denied you?" Andrew asked, his heart breaking.

"The man who offered for me told my father that you were going on a fool-hardy mission," she said. "That you would not be returning."

"That's a lie," Andrew spat. "We are only going to Morganna's castle to find a document. On the appointed day we would leave at first light and be back by midday."

She snuggled against him. "But, my love, that is so dangerous," she said. "Surely you are not going alone?"

"Oh, well, I could do it by myself," he boasted. "But, no, there will be five of us. And Sir Tristan will be leading our quest. There is no finer knight than he."

She gasped softly.

"What? What is it my darling?" he asked.

"He's the one who offered for me," she whispered, her voice breaking with grief.

"Who?" Andrew asked.

"Tristan," she whispered softly. "Tristan paid for me."

Andrew released her and stumbled backwards, shaking his head. "No," he said in shock. "No. Tristan knew how I felt about you. Tristan told me to go to your father. No."

"I heard it myself," she replied. "They were laughing about some poor fool…" She gasped again. "Oh, no, they wouldn't have been laughing about you."

"Laughing…at me?" he whispered. "That can't be right. That can't be true."

"You know I would not lie to you, Andrew," she whispered. "What good would it bring me?"

He stumbled back, away from her, shaking his head. Finally, his heart broken by the betrayal of his idol, Sir Andrew turned and blindly rushed out of the stables.

The young woman walked slowly to the door and watched as the young knight slopped through the ice-cold mud on his way back towards the inn. A smile spread on her lips, and Morganna finally laughed out loud. She reached up and pulled her bloodstone amulet out from beneath her apron. Stroking it gently, she felt its power thrum beneath her hand. "Thank you for your assistance, young knight," she laughed, watching Andrew stumble forward in the storm. "I look forward to seeing you on the morrow."

Chapter Seven

The hour was well past midnight when Tristan was awakened by soft knocks on his chamber door. Grabbing his sword, he hurried over to the door.

"Your name?" he whispered.

"Garrett," came the gruff and impatiently reply. "Now open the door."

Tristan laid his sword against the wall and slipped the bolt from the lock on the door. "What do you…"

Garrett shook his head to silence him. "I've received word from one who is not a loyal follower of Morganna that on the morrow at low tide she leaves her castle," he whispered.

Tristan was immediately awake. "This seems far too favorable a coincidence," he replied softly. "Do you suspect a trap?"

Garrett smiled ironically. "I always suspect a trap," he said. "And yes, this indeed might be a wily snare. But if Morganna has discovered what we intend to do, we might as well act quickly and try to find the scroll than allow her henchmen to kill us in our sleep."

Nodding slowly, Tristan met Garrett's eyes. "We only have three hours to low tide," he said. "You must wake the others and meet me in the woods a half league from her castle."

"And where are you going?" Garrett asked suspiciously.

Tristan pulled his tunic over his head and pulled his belt around his waist. "I'm off to wake a wizard from his sleep," he replied. "Pray I don't end up with two heads."

Garrett laughed softly. "Well, perhaps the extra one will have more brains in it," he replied. "Godspeed. We will meet you by dawn in the woods."

Garrett slipped quietly out into the hallway and hurried down the hall, knocking on the next door. He smiled as he heard the groaning of the wooden bed as the occupant rolled out of it. Rufus was probably having a fitful night sleep as it was, considering his girth and the typical size of one of the beds in this inn.

The door opened, and a sleepy Rufus stared at Garrett through blurry eyes. "Aye?" he asked, his voice thick.

"We need to leave, now," Garrett said, enjoying waking his friend more than he should.

A thick, red eyebrow raised, and green eyes, now clear, stared back at Garrett. "Now?" he asked, displeasure in his voice.

Garrett nodded and leaned forward, lowering his voice. "Morganna leaves her castle at low tide," he whispered. "We are to meet Tristan at the edge of the forest nearest her castle."

"Give me a moment," Rufus said soberly and closed the door on Garrett's face.

With a nonchalant shrug, Garrett traveled farther down the hall to knock on the next door. It took no time to wake Duncan and hasten his preparations. Now he only had Andrew to deal with.

He knocked on the door a little harder than the rest, hoping to startle the young knight. But the visage that stood in front of him when the door was opened surprised even the hardened Garrett.

"Are you sick, whifling," he asked.

"What do you want?" Andrew asked belligerently, the smell of strong spirits apparent.

Garrett stepped through the doorway and grabbed the young man by the collar of his nightclothes, closing the door behind him. "You agree to be part of a quest, and then you become so piss-poor drunk that we can't even use you?" he growled menacingly. "If you were so fearful that you needed to get your courage from a bottle, you should not have agreed to come."

Andrew flailed his fists around in the direction of Garrett but was unable to land a punch. "I am not afraid," he yelled with a marked slur to his voice. "I'm not afraid of you or of Tristan or of Morganna."

Garrett tightened his grip on Andrew's collar. "Lower your voice," he demanded, his low voice harsh and clipped. "Have you lost all reason?"

Andrew shuddered, and tears filled his eyes. "I've lost my heart," he admitted sadly.

Garrett pushed Andrew back, so he fell onto the bed. "And I told you countless times that women were not to be trusted. They are fine enough company to keep your bed warm, but never, ever trust them with your heart," he growled through clenched teeth.

Andrew shook his head. "It wasn't her fault," he cried. "Her father sold her off to the highest bidder. She was betrayed." He shook his head and lowered his voice. "We were both betrayed."

Garrett looked around the room and spied the pile of clothing unceremoniously dumped on the table near the door. He strode over, picked up the clothing and threw them at the young knight. "I can't leave you here in your current state of intoxication. You would more than likely tell anyone about our mission," he spat. "So, like it or not, you are riding with us. You have three minutes to get dressed."

Andrew struggled to sit up. "I don't want to go," he whined. "I don't want to be part of this quest."

Garrett withdrew his sword from his scabbard and pointed it at the young man. "Either you come with us or I diminish your ability to tell any tales," he said, staring at Andrew with cold, cruel eyes.

Andrew swallowed loudly and nodded.

"Three minutes," Garrett reminded him and then swept from the room.

Chapter Eight

Merlin stood at the tower window gazing out over the forest and beyond to Camelot. Tristan, standing several feet behind him, waited patiently for the wizard to speak. Finally, after releasing a sad sigh, the old man turned to the young knight.

"You are sure Morganna has a spell that would destroy Camelot?" he asked.

Tristan nodded. "Aye, Duncan the scholar studied the information I had and felt that it could destroy any chance Camelot had of regaining her strength."

Merlin walked away from the window, his long robes dragging on the stone floor. He finally stopped and turned to Tristan, his eyes blazing. "I am not powerless, you know," he stated.

Nodding, Tristan took a tentative step forward. "You, Merlin, are the greatest of wizards," he paused and took a deep breath. "But even your power is limited."

Merlin stiffened and glared at Tristan. "Most men would not have lived after speaking those words. But I grant you a pardon, knowing that you are not yourself."

His heart pounding in his chest, Tristan bit his tongue, waiting for the wizard's anger to calm. He watched the wizened man pace across the floor several times and then finally come to a stop in front of the globe of the world resting on a tall, wooden stand. Idly spinning the globe with one finger, Merlin looked calm, but Tristan was not fooled.

Finally, the wizard turned and looked at the knight. "I am not limited," he growled concisely. "And you would do well to remember that."

Tristan walked over to Merlin and met his eyes. "Limited by your ethics," Tristan explained. "What you will and will not do, rather than what you cannot do."

Merlin spun the globe again. "And this spell that Morganna has—what can she do that you believe I cannot stop?"

Reaching beyond Merlin, Tristan put his hand on the globe to stop its forward motion. Then he spun it in reverse. "She can change time, Merlin," he said. "She can move to the past and the future. She can be in all places, know all outcomes, and change the things she doesn't like."

Stunned, Merlin turned quickly, knocking the globe over and sending it rolling across the stone floor of his chamber. "But...but there is great danger using that kind of power," the wizard stammered. "Great danger indeed. Why, the whole course of human life could be altered!"

Tristan walked across the room and picked up the globe now lying against a wall in the corner of the room. He came back to Merlin and carefully replaced the globe on its stand and then turned to face the wizard. "Will you help me?" he asked.

Merlin sighed and nodded. "You were right, my boy," he replied sadly. "I do have my limits, much as I am loathe to admit it. I do not have the power to protect you from Morganna's spells should she catch you."

Tristan nodded and bowed slightly. "Thank you for your time," he said and turned to walk away.

But a gnarled, claw-like hand on his shoulder halted his progression.

"Wait, Sir Tristan," Merlin said. "I do not have the power to protect you fully, but I can place a charm over you and the rest of the knights, so she will not be able to kill you." He shrugged. "I know it's not much…"

"It's more than I had when I entered your chamber," Tristan replied. "Thank you, Merlin."

Merlin smiled sadly. "You are welcome, young knight," he replied. "And should she place another kind of spell on you, come to me, and I will see what I can do."

"I will," Tristan replied, feeling hopeful. "But we need not worry. We are going to search her belongings when she is gone from her lair."

Chapter Nine

She was beautiful; dark, ebony hair fell past her shoulders in lustrous curls, past a wide, sensuous mouth with blood-hued lips and skin as white as fresh-fallen snow. But her eyes told the true story of the Lady Morganna. Her eyes held the darkness of graveyards at midnight, the anger of a storm-tossed sea, and the heartlessness of a piece of obsidian, black and hard.

Standing at the tower of her castle, she looked down on the village of Camelot, a rare smile forming on her lips. The place was in ruin, the people demoralized and the king a mere shadow of his former self. *Yes*, she thought, *things are going very well.*

Turning from the window, she hurried back to the long, wooden table where her philter was brewing over a small fire enclosed in an earthen pot. Leaning over, she waved her hand over the top of the potion, moving the steam towards her and inhaling deeply. It smelled like death—rotting, fermenting, oozing corpses. Her smile widened. It was nearly perfect.

She picked up an empty cobalt bottle, placed it close to the brewing potion and put a funnel into its narrow opening. Using silver tongs, she lifted the potion, poured it into the bottle, and sealed it with a cork stopper.

"Now, let's see," she said, placing her finger to her lip. "Brew the potion, let cool and allow to age for more potency. A week is not nearly enough. A month will give you a localized plague, and a year could destroy an entire kingdom."

She wrapped the bottle in a cloth and lifted it up to her face. "But what would one thousand years accomplish?" she whispered. "I could destroy the world with you, my dear, little potion."

She placed the potion back on the table and walked across the room to a tall table that stood in the center of a pentagram drawn on the floor. A large, leather-bound book sat on the table, but Morganna pushed it to the side to uncover a small secret compartment. She lifted the top panel and pulled out an ancient scroll. Tenderly unwrapping it, she scanned down the page, whispering the words of the spell as she held tightly to her bloodstone amulet.

Then she wrapped the scroll back up, placed it back in the hidden compartment and slid the book back over the top.

She scooped the potion into her arms and strode towards the door. "I need my carriage immediately!" she screamed, and those who served her ran to do her bidding.

The tide was just falling when the spacious black carriage sprang from the courtyard and thundered across the isthmus towards the road that led to Avalon.

They traveled only a few miles away from the castle before Morganna rapped sharply on the roof of the carriage, demanding they stop. The driver pulled the carriage off the road into a nearby forest and alighted, awaiting his mistress's pleasure. She violently pushed open the door, slamming it against the outside of the carriage, and tapped her foot impatiently while her henchmen hurried to help her out. Clutching the cloth-wrapped bottle in her hand, she walked to the edge of the forest and then turned to her men. "Wait here for me," she ordered.

The woods were calm and quiet, and the setting moon cast light down the path she walked. She trod quickly down the dirt path, so intent on her destination that she paid little attention to the woodland creatures that scurried to get out of her way. Finally, she arrived at her destination, a young yew tree. She placed the bottle into a small cleft in the base of the tree and stepped back with a smile. "Let's see how long you endure, young yew," she said.

She closed her eyes, held tightly to her amulet and pictured the yew massive and old, hundreds of years in the future. Then she whispered the words of the spell.

Wind whipped around her, creating a vortex that swirled through time. The seasons melded together. Starlight and sunlight, moons and clouds followed each other across the sky, and the young tree grew and aged before her eyes. Tender green leaves turned brittle and brown in a moment, then returned to blossom again. Finally, the wind slowed, day and night became more apparent in their transitions, and she could feel the difference in the changes of weather as they hurried past. Then, all was silent.

Morganna looked around. The woods had changed; the village had now expanded to claim it as part of the square. The yew was now in the courtyard of an inn. She stepped forward and approached the old tree. "Now let's see what we have here," she exclaimed, waving her hand and causing the trunk of the tree to part. She knelt down and reached into the fissure and withdrew the cobalt bottle, with only tiny remnants of the cloth clinging to it.

Pleased, she allowed a smile to cross her face. "I believe this calls for a celebration," she decided and turned and walked towards the inn.

The taproom was dark and musty, smelling of aged liquor and smoked wood. She approached the bartender and smiled sweetly. "I'm afraid I'm a stranger in these parts," she said. "Is it appropriate for a lady to have a drink in your establishment?"

A gruff and brawny man seated at the bar turned to her. "I'm the magistrate in these parts," he boasted. "And what I say goes."

Smiling at him, she lowered her lashes flirtatiously. "And what do you say, Sir Magistrate?"

He leered back. "Aloysius. Aloysius Murphy. I say it's appropriate for you to have a drink if you are drinking with me," he replied, standing and bowing slightly. "Thomas, bring some wine to the table in the corner. That's where this fine lady and me are going to relax."

Morganna smiled. "How kind of you," she replied, slipping her hand around his arm. "And perhaps you can tell me about your little community. You never know when something learned could be of great import."

Chapter Ten

Tristan urged his horse on when he spied his fellow knights waiting just inside the shelter of the woods. He galloped into their midst and pulled his horse up next to Garrett's steed.

"Well met, friends," he said, slightly out of breath. "I have just come from Merlin's tower, and he has gifted us all with these amulets. They hold enough power that Morganna cannot end our lives."

He pulled the amulets with their leather thongs from the inside of his tunic and handed one to each of the men.

Andrew pulled his horse away when Tristan approached him. "I don't need it," Andrew snapped angrily.

"Andrew?" Tristan asked, concerned. "What's wrong?"

"Nothing a good night's sleep and the hair of the dog wouldn't fix," Garrett replied snidely.

"You're drunk?" Tristan asked, shocked. "But, Andrew, you agreed to this quest. You know…"

Andrew turned back, his eyes glaring with anger. "What? Don't you dare tell me that I know the knight's code, that I know the oath we all took— bravery, courtesy, honor and great gallantry toward women. What about loyalty, Tristan? What about truth?"

Tristan shook his head. "Andrew, truly, I have done nothing to have you doubt my loyalty or my honesty towards you."

"Have you not?" Andrew began.

"Leave the boy be," Rufus said, nosing his large steed between the other two. He turned to Andrew. "I heard about your lass last night, and I'm sorry for you."

Tristan turned to Rufus. "What? What did you hear?"

"The Lady Anwyn was found floating in the river, just before the woods," Rufus said. "By all accounts, she was murdered."

Andrew shook his head. "No, she can't be," he stammered. "When? When did you hear this?"

"I heard the news as we were leaving the inn last night," Rufus replied. "One of the men in the tavern shared the tale. He was there when her father identified her body."

Shocked, Andrew turned from Rufus to Tristan. "No!" he said, shaking his head. "No, that can't be right. I saw her—"

"There's movement on the castle grounds. They are preparing to leave," Garrett called out, halting all conversation.

Tristan pushed an amulet into Andrew's hand. "Wear it," he said. "You have much to live for. If nothing else, to avenge the death of your beloved."

"But, I…Tristan, I need to tell you…" he began.

Tristan placed his hand on Andrew's upper arm and nodded encouragingly. "Whatever it is, Sir Andrew, it will have to wait until we finish this quest," he replied.

He turned and rode back to the edge of the forest to watch alongside Garrett.

The wet sand of the isthmus appeared from beneath the water, like a sea serpent rising from the deep, and within minutes Morganna and her black carriage, pulled by six powerful, black horses, thundered across the narrow passage and onward through the woods.

"We don't know how long she'll be gone, lads," Tristan said. "Let's ride as if our lives depend on it."

Tristan and his compatriots urged their horses forward, and in minutes they were traversing the self-same path Morganna had just ridden. They galloped through the wet sand, galloping hooves sending a spray of sand into the sky, and pulled their steeds to a halt in the dark castle's courtyard.

Garrett trotted his horse around the circumference of the courtyard. "She has left no guards to protect her lair," he said quietly. "This does not bode well."

Duncan looked around slowly. "Perhaps she felt that no one would think of entering her castle," he reasoned. "Quite frankly, this is the last place I would choose to be."

"Well, trap or no," Tristan said, "it's an opportunity to discover the spell. So, swords at the ready in case there are some surprises to deal with."

Chapter Eleven

The knights leapt from their horses and ran to the castle entrance. Tristan took the lead with Rufus at his back. Duncan and Andrew followed, with Garrett taking up the rear. They pushed open the huge, oak doors and ran into the large main hall.

Large, dark tapestries depicting scenes of horror and dark magic hung from the stone walls all along the circumference of the circular room. Long, wooden tables ran along each side of the room, one after another, until there were enough spaces to easily seat two hundred. At the back of the room, one long table was on a raised dais, elevating it several feet above the other tables in the room, and behind it sat a throne, upholstered in black and purple velvet.

"Just like home," Rufus mocked. "If home were an asylum."

"We don't have time to gape like country bumpkins," Garrett said sharply. "Let's get going."

They began to climb the tall, stone staircase that was attached to the outer wall of the castle.

Tristan ran up the stairs, his sword before him, looking for any guards who would bar their way.

Strange symbols had been painted on the wooden beams that crossed over their heads and above the windows.

"What are those?" Andrew asked, his voice shaking.

"Protective symbols," Garrett replied, pushing the young man forward.

"Why are they painted in red?" the young knight asked.

"Because that's the color of the blood they used," Garrett replied harshly. "And I, for one, would rather not have my blood smeared onto the walls of Morganna's castle, so hurry up these stairs!"

They reached the second floor and ran down the hall to a large room whose doors stood open.

"I don't like this at all," Garrett said.

"I don't either," Tristan agreed. "But we must take the cards we're dealt."

Morganna's chamber was filled with macabre trophies of her association with black magic. Potions

64

bubbled in small, black cauldrons sitting next to shelves full of glass jars that held the grisly ingredients of her next philter. Tristan shuddered at the large, decomposing finger floating in some clear liquid inside one of the jars.

"Dead man's finger," Garrett whispered to him. "Useful for many spells in the black arts."

"I really didn't need to know that," Tristan replied, moving away from the disgusting display.

Amulets and crystals hung from silver chains and jangled discordantly in the light breeze that swept through the windows.

Other shelves held leather bound books with spells from all over the world. In the corner of the room sat a large canopy with veiling reminiscent of burial shrouds.

The knights paused in the middle of the room, nearly overcome by the evil atmosphere of the room. "There's no time to waste, laddies," Rufus roared. "We must be in and out of here quickly."

"Duncan, will you stand at the window and be the lookout?" Tristan asked. "We don't want to be caught unaware."

"As you wish, Sir Tristan," Duncan replied, hurrying to the narrow window that overlooked the front of the castle.

The rest of the knights spread throughout the room and began carefully searching each shelf, drawer and hidden panel they could find.

In the middle of the room, a tall table stood with an ancient text upon it. Tristan decided to start his search there. Hurrying to the table, he started to reach for the book when someone grabbed his arm to stop him.

"That is the Black Grimoire," Garrett said, stepping closer alongside Tristan. "There is as much evil within the pages of that book as Morganna holds in her heart. You would do well not to touch it."

Garrett lifted his sword, pushed the old book to the side, and uncovered a small, hinged panel.

"This must be the place," Tristan exclaimed and quickly unlocked it. Pushing the panel up, he found several dozen rolled scrolls lying next to each other. Both men reached in, grabbed a scroll, and began scanning the words to discover if they held the correct parchment.

"Gentleman," Duncan called from the window, "there is a cloud of dust coming through the forest in this direction. If I'm not mistaken, it is Morganna's carriage."

"How much time do we have?" Tristan asked.

Duncan stared out the window for a long moment. "Well, taking into account the velocity of the coach, the fatigue of her team, the drag of the wheels through the sand…"

"How much?" Tristan demanded.

Duncan turned to Tristan. "Only a wee bit of time, milord," he said. "I would suggest we hurry."

"We have to leave!" Andrew shouted. "We have to leave now, or she'll catch us."

Tristan turned to his men.

"I cannot dictate your decisions," he said. "She is close, and we may be caught if we linger. I, for one, will stay until I find the document."

Rufus shrugged and went back to haphazardly pulling drawers out of a dresser and emptying them onto the floor. "I'll stay. I would hate to have spent this time for naught."

Duncan chuckled softly. "I'll stay," he said. "I tend to always miss the good adventures."

Andrew looked from the stairs back to Tristan. His forehead was beaded in sweat, and his hands were shaking. He took a deep breath. "I'll stay too," he stammered.

"Good man," Tristan said to him with a smile. Then Tristan turned to Garrett, who stood at his side, still pulling the scrolls out of the table.

"If you even ask me if I'm staying," Garrett whispered, "I'll run you through with my sword."

Tristan smiled and nodded. "I wouldn't dream of it," he said, pulling out another scroll.

"She is nearing the edge of the woods," Duncan called out. "She has yet to cross the causeway."

Pulling out a large drawer, Rufus lifted it up and unceremoniously dumped it on the floor, shattering some of the contents inside. "Ach, what a shame," Rufus said. "It seems I might have damaged some of the lady's trinkets."

"She's going to kill you," Andrew stammered.

"And there's the beauty of it," Rufus replied. "She cannot kill us." He paused for a moment. "Although, truth to tell, I'd as soon be dead than turned into one of these trophies on her wall."

"Hopefully none of that will be necessary," Tristan called out, shoving a scroll into his tunic. "I've found the spell."

"Throw the others back into the table quickly," Garrett ordered, "so she doesn't realize that we found her hiding spot."

They took valuable moments to put the table back together, sliding the Black Grimoire back in place with their swords.

"Now run," Tristan said, leading the way to the hall.

"Leaving so soon, milords?" Morganna asked, slowly coming up the staircase towards them. "Oh.

No. You must stay. I insist. I have not yet fulfilled my duties as a hostess."

Chapter Twelve

Garrett stepped around Tristan and faced Morganna. "Milady," he said softly, nodding at her.

"Sir Garrett," Morganna gasped, losing her composure for a moment.

Garrett met her eyes unflinchingly. "You need to move out of the way," he ordered.

Her eyes narrowed, and the softness was immediately gone. "I think not," she replied. She waved her hand, and Garrett was thrown backwards into her chamber. "I believe there are things we must discuss."

She moved forward, and the knights, with their swords drawn, retreated back into the chamber.

"Let them go," Tristan said. "I instigated this attack on your castle. They are innocent."

She laughed bitterly. "Why would I let them go when in an instant I can just kill you all where you stand?"

She lifted both her hands over her head and whispered the words to a spell. Sparks flew from one hand to the other. Then the sparks formed strings of electricity that gathered together to form a blazing orb of energy. She smiled at the knights. "So much for the knights of the Round Table," she mocked, and then she threw the orb at them.

Energy sizzled and sparked, creating a blue haze in the room, but when it cleared, the knights still stood in the middle of the room—very much alive.

"What is this?" she screamed. "Why are you not dead?"

"You can't hurt us," Andrew yelled out. "Merlin is protecting us."

Garrett cuffed the young knight on the head. "You idiot," he whispered angrily.

Morganna smiled and nodded at Andrew. "Thank you, once again, young knight," she replied.

"Once again?" Rufus asked, turning to Andrew, his voice filled with rage. "Once again?"

"Aye, the young cub betrayed you," Morganna laughed. "But secrets will be whispered when you're in the midst of passion."

Andrew shook his head. "She tricked me," he pleaded to the men around him. "She pretended she was Anwyn, pretended she loved me…"

His voice shook, and then he took a deep breath. "No," he continued sadly. "I am at fault. I betrayed your confidence. I broke the oath. There is no one to blame but myself."

Garrett sighed. "We often make great mistakes when we believe ourselves in love," he said. Then he looked at Morganna. "Do we not, milady?"

"Not everything was a mistake, Sir Garrett," she replied.

He shook his head. "You're wrong," he said harshly. "Every moment was a mistake."

Glaring at him, she clenched her teeth and lifted her arms again, power surging between her hands. "Merlin has the power to deny me the ability to kill you where you stand," she finally said. "But he has no power over my other spells. And so, my good knights, I pronounce on you my aging spell. For every day you live as a man, you will age a decade. In a week, you will have gained seventy years. In a fortnight, you will be resting in your graves."

She threw the brilliant orb at them, and it washed over their bodies, illuminating them momentarily then moving on until it dissipated at the back of her chamber.

She looked over her chamber, noting the upturned drawers and the emptied shelves. But when her eyes rested on the Black Grimoire still in place and the table seemingly untouched, she smiled triumphantly.

"And now I will grant you your request, Sir Garrett," she taunted. "I will gladly move out of your way, as it seems your quest here was for naught."

She stepped to the side and bowed slightly. "Good day, sir knights."

Tristan moved past her quickly, and the other knights followed. They were silent until they had mounted their horses and were traveling back across the isthmus.

"Where to now, laddie?" Rufus asked Tristan.

"To Merlin," he said. "To see what he can do to alter her spell."

Chapter Thirteen

Merlin met the knights at the base of his tower, shaking his head with regret. "I'm so sorry," he called to them as they stopped their steeds next to him. "I didn't think that she would or could do anything as devious as that spell she placed upon you."

"You know what she did?" Tristan asked as he dismounted.

Merlin nodded. "I watched a portion through my scrying bowl. I saw that Morganna caught you and that you were not successful in your quest."

"That's what we wanted Morganna to believe," Tristan said, pulling the scroll out from beneath his tunic. "It was Sir Garrett's idea. He thought to buy us more time."

Merlin took the scroll from Tristan and carried it to a large stump of an old oak tree. The stump was the size of a table, and the surface was smooth and level. He rolled open the scroll and placed smooth stones on each corner to hold it in place. Then he bent over the document and studied it carefully.

"This is a powerful incantation," he said slowly. "And one that will not be easy to reverse."

"But it can be reversed?" Tristan asked.

Merlin nodded slowly, his eyes still on the parchment. "This is not a mere spell, but because it is associated with time, it will be a quest," he explained. "You must travel as far in time as Morganna to stop her. And once you stop her, I will be able to bring you back to Camelot as if you'd never left."

"Well, from the spell she put on us, we have a week to live," Garrett replied. "So, I suggest you look for another group to go on your quest."

Merlin shook his head. "No, you have already put into motion the first steps of the quest," he said. "It has to be you."

"But how?" Duncan asked. "Morganna's spell was specific. For every day we live as men, we will age a decade."

Merlin looked over at Duncan and raised one, shaggy eyebrow. "Who says you have to live as men?" he asked.

"What?" Tristan asked.

"First things first," Merlin said, shaking his head impatiently and turning back to the parchment. "Once you start on your quest, you will need to acquire two things. First, remember the phrase, nobile viri pura cordis incantatores conteram."

"A man, pure of heart, will break the spell," Duncan translated. "Surely as knights we are pure of heart."

"Not all of us," Garrett remarked softly.

"It means more than that," Merlin said. "It would be too easy if it were merely a good-hearted man. No, this is far more precise. It is not just a characteristic. It is a heritage."

"Do you mean a part of his name?" Tristan suggested. "Is there a family name that means pure of heart?"

"Aye, the Herdin line," Rufus replied. "Their family line goes back hundreds of years."

"So, you must seek out a member of that family to help you on your quest," Merlin agreed. "And then, the other item you need to break the spell is something powerful and precious owned by the one who cast the spell."

"There is nothing precious to Morganna," Andrew inserted. "She loves only herself."

Garrett shook his head. "Her bloodstone amulet," he said with conviction. "There is nothing she treasures more than her amulet. It is never off her person."

"You should know," Andrew mocked snidely.

Garrett turned quickly and drew his sword. "You may live another week, or I can end your life here and now," he growled softly.

Tristan stepped between Garrett and Andrew, pushing the tip of Garrett's sword toward the ground. "Andrew, you will apologize to Sir Garrett," he said firmly. "If not for Garrett, we would never have made it out of Morganna's castle."

Andrew stared obstinately at Garrett for a few long moments, then sighed and nodded. "I apologize,

Sir Garrett," he finally replied. "My comment was rude and childish. I am in no place to judge any man's actions."

Garrett sheathed his sword and nodded at the young knight. "Your apology is accepted," he said. Then he turned to Merlin. "And now that first things first are out of the way, how do you intend to keep us from aging prematurely?"

Chapter Fourteen

Merlin stroked his long beard as he contemplated Garrett's question. "The spell was quite specific," he mused. "For every day you live as men, you will age a decade."

"And we aren't getting any younger standing here with you," Rufus complained. When Merlin turned to him with angry, steely eyes, the giant, red-headed knight took several steps backward. "Begging your pardon, your Wizardship."

"I do realize there's a time element, Sir Rufus," Merlin replied tersely. "But we must carefully consider your options. Whatever form I change you into will need to accommodate your varied needs. A butterfly, though mobile, is too delicate and fragile to last. A field mouse, though discreet and resourceful, can be killed by a swipe of a chambermaid's broom."

"We will assume the characteristics of the creatures we embody?" Tristan asked.

Merlin nodded slowly. "Yes, I believe you will," he said.

"Then we must find creatures who will run in packs or herds," Tristan replied, "so we instinctively stay together."

Smiling in approval, Merlin nodded. "Well done, Sir Tristan," he said. "Yes, we must be sure you are beasts who travel together."

"And ones who are not foe to man," Rufus added. "We cannot be wolves and expect to survive among farmers."

"Aye," Tristan agreed. "And it would be better if our appetites were for things we could forage in the meadows and woods than if we needed flesh to satisfy our needs."

"But no prize stags," Garrett added. "I'd lief as not have my head hanging above some mantle in a country squire's estate."

"Valid point, Sir Garrett," Merlin agreed. "So, if we have eliminated creatures who eat flesh and creatures who are valued for both meat and trophy, what have we left?"

Tristan glanced over his shoulder to the knights' steeds who were grazing together in the sparse patch of grass next to the wizard's tower.

"Horses," Tristan said thoughtfully. "Horses can travel long distances, can eat from the meadows and woods, are not hunted for sport and will travel together in a herd."

"As long as we're not geldings," Rufus said with a loud guffaw. "I'll give up much, but not that."

Merlin chuckled softly. "Aye, Sir Rufus, that would be asking too much, even for knights of the Round Table." He turned to Tristan. "Horses it is, young knight. Are you ready?"

It was all moving far too quickly for the young knight. He had so many unanswered questions. So many concerns.

"Wait!" Tristan cried urgently. "Before you turn us to steeds, where shall we go? Who shall we find?"

"Find the one who can help you break the spell," Merlin advised. "Find a warrior from the Herdin line. That is all I can tell you."

Rufus patted Tristan's back reassuringly. "Not a problem," Rufus exclaimed. "It's a day's journey to the Herdin estate, a day to break the spell and then another day's return trip. We'll be back by week's end."

Merlin shook his head sadly. "I feel in my heart that your journey will be long and hard," he replied. "You will witness the folly and greed of men. You will see what corruption can do to a soul. But, I also believe that you will see goodness, generosity, loyalty and love. And these things above all will make your journey worthwhile."

The knights were silent, each absorbing Merlin's pronouncement.

"How long?" Tristan finally asked.

"I cannot say," the wizard answered. "But for those of you who leave family behind, understand that I will watch over and protect them. They will want for nothing, except your companionship, while you are gone."

Rufus turned away from his companions and walked to the edge of the hill that Merlin's tower stood upon. From there he could see past the forest to the city of Camelot. He stared at the city, trying to discern from this distance where his home lay.

"Rufus?" Tristan asked, coming up beside him.

"I kissed them goodnight before I left for our meeting," he said, his voice hoarse and broken. "I told them I loved them more than life itself." He took a shuddering breath. "It will have to do. It will have to do until I return."

"And because we'll have broken the spell, we'll return back to today, so they won't miss you at all," Tristan said.

"But I'll miss them every moment I'm away," Rufus replied. He took a deep breath and then turned to Tristan. "Well then, let's be off so we can be home all the sooner. Let's go find the Herdin warrior."

Chapter Fifteen

Morganna hurried up the stone steps to the tower where she performed her spells and created her potions. She paused before entering the room and listened carefully. Only a few days prior she had come across a handful of Arthur's finest trying to hinder her plans, and she did not want that distraction today. Hearing nothing, she pushed open the door and entered the chamber, hurrying to the table in the middle of the room. She slipped off the bloodied apron and laid it on one of the tables. She was pleased that she had enough blood to perform another seeking spell if she needed it.

She washed her hands in another bowl filled with water, quickly dried them, and reached back into her pocket for the narrow, black runes. They had been right, according to the signs that had been provided by her latest divination. There was a threat to her and her power coming from a future time period—a threat she would have to put an end to.

"Show me," she cried out as she tossed the runes onto the table before her.

Leaning over, she studied the symbols etched into the black rock. Once again, the runes showed the danger came from the future.

"The future holds no threat to me now," she whispered, her eyes narrowed in concentration. "Nothing can threaten me now!"

She hurried across the room to the tall, narrow desk that held her Black Grimoire, her book of spells. She shoved the grimoire to the side and opened the trap door beneath with a snap. Shoving aside other parchments, she searched wildly for the newest spell—the time travel spell. But it was nowhere to be found.

Her heart dropped. Whoever had the spell held the ability to reverse it and retract her abilities.

"Those knights," she screamed, lifting her head and driving the sound throughout the castle. "Find me those knights!"

She could hear the scurry of her servants as they hurried from the castle to do her bidding, but she wasn't satisfied.

"They could be anywhere," she whispered. "Merlin could have sent them anywhere."

She smiled, remembering the spell she'd placed upon them.

"Move them anywhere you would like, wizard," she laughed. "They can grow decrepit and senile away from Camelot too."

Suddenly, a sixth sense had her turning to see a large snowy owl perched on the edge of her window. It stared at her calmly, no fear registering in its eyes…

Its eyes!

Not the eyes of a bird but the eyes of a man stared back at her.

"Merlin!" she screamed. "What have you done?"

With a mocking bow and the hint of humor in its eyes, the giant bird lifted off its perch and flew away from the tower.

Shouting an oath of frustration, she crossed the room and picked up the bloodied apron and wrung it out, leaving a small pool of blood in a bowl.

Lifting the bowl, she crossed the room to a small, hidden, narrow staircase that wrapped around the outer edge of the rounded tower room and made its way to a small loft. Climbing the stairs, she stepped into a small, round chamber with the pointed peak of the castle only a few feet over her head. There were thirteen windows cut into the stone, all equally distanced from each other. The floor was polished wood, and a red pentagram was inlaid into the flooring from wall to wall.

In the center of the pentagram was a gnarled and twisted piece of wood about four feet tall and two feet in diameter. The wood was so finely polished the golden tones glowed. The lower part of the piece had thick tendrils, like roots, sticking out in every direction to form a stable base. The top had branches sticking out symmetrically in every direction and held a silver scrying bowl. The outside of the bowl was ornately carved with each quadrant representing one of the seasons of the year. The inside was polished smooth and filled with pure water.

Morganna stood over the bowl and dripped some of the blood into the clear water. Instantly, the water began to foam, and a gray mist bubbled over the sides of the bowl, pouring onto the floor.

Morganna lifted her hands above her head and threw back her head. She whispered the words of the spell while the room darkened, and the wind rushed around her. The gray mist moved with the wind, twirling around the room, climbing up to cover the walls and windows, and rising to the ceiling. Finally, the room was completely filled with gray, murky fog except for the area just around Morganna and the bowl. She lowered her head, her eyes now a glowing, verdant green, and looked down into the bowl.

The bubbling stopped, and the mist inside the bowl dissipated. Morganna could see a picture forming before her.

She recognized the yew tree in the courtyard of the inn she had visited earlier. The view changed and moved, as if she were walking in the small village. It took her down the main road out of town and then up to the top of a hill. A gypsy camp was laid out before her with a number of wagons forming a circle of protection. Then the view changed again, as if she were turning around and viewing what was on the other side of the hill.

A mansion built of pink-beige stone lay a mile below her. It was surrounded by lush gardens and a tidy stable. There was activity around the house, mostly servants hurrying to and fro in the gardens and back into the main house. As she watched the house, the gray mist seemed to seep back up from the floor and roll over the grounds of the mansion.

"So, this is where the threat lays," Morganna whispered, a wicked smile spreading across her face. "Well, we shall just have to take care of that, won't we?"

Chapter Sixteen

Lady Meaghan Isolde Herdin stood on the edge of a bluff, overlooking the ruins of what used to be her family home. The wind whipped wickedly against her, and the colorful cotton dress and coarse, handspun shawl, a gift from the gypsies, did nothing to ward away the damp chill of the day. The acrid scent of smoke was still carried by the wind although it had been a week since Morganna had conjured a massive bolt of electricity and sent it hurling into the estate, killing everyone inside.

She turned and could see the small graveyard where members of her family had been buried for centuries. Now three freshly-turned gravesites lay side by side in the far corner. There lay her mother, her father and her sweet chambermaid, Daisy, whom everyone assumed was Meaghan because of her gift of a rose-colored dress.

Meaghan sighed, brushed away the errant tears in her eyes, and wrapped the shawl more tightly around her body.

"Are you not afraid of being seen?"

She looked over her shoulder to find Jepson, her father's trusted friend, standing directly behind her. His face still showed the bruises and abrasions from his encounter with the magistrate and his ruffians a week earlier. Meaghan sighed and shrugged.

"People see what they expect to see," she said sadly. "Lady Meaghan is dead. They will not suspect a lone gypsy woman."

"But Morganna…" Jepson began.

Meaghan's eyes changed in an instant from grief-stricken to incensed. "Let her come," she said, her voice low and ominous. "There is much I wish to say and do to Morganna."

Jepson stepped alongside Meaghan and winced as he moved, the pain to his broken ribs still apparent. He looked down at that same scene and lowered his voice. "And while you are caught up in your anger and your grief, she will have the advantage," he said softly. "A cool and calculating head is always the best when dealing with an adversary."

"How do you stop the anger? How do you end the grief?" she whispered.

He placed his hand on her shoulder and sighed softly. "The grief will not end. It will always be your companion as you journey forward," he said. "But your choice will be to either allow this companion to lead your journey or for you to take charge."

"And the anger?" she asked.

"Ah, well, that is harder," he said. "You are justified in your anger and condemnation of Morganna. She is evil, heartless, and vindictive."

Meaghan nodded. "Yes, she is," she agreed. "All that and more."

Jepson was silent a moment while he gathered his thoughts. Finally, he spoke. "The very last thing you want to do is allow the anger and the desire for retribution to fester in your heart and change the person you are."

She turned to him. "She deserves punishment," she insisted. "She killed my parents."

He met her eyes and nodded slowly. "Yes, she does," he said. "But are you the one to mete out her punishment, or do you leave it to a greater power?"

She shook her head, clearly confused. "What do you mean?"

"There is a power greater than us all. A power that uses both justice and mercy when judging the actions of others," he explained. "If we leave revenge to that power, having faith in this all-seeing and all-knowing authority, then we are free of the burden of hate and anger."

"I don't know if I have that much faith," she murmured, turning back to look at the graveyard.

"Then, perhaps, you need to lean on the faith of your parents," he said softly. "What would they have you do?"

She stared at the graveyard, and tears filled her eyes. Impatiently, she wiped them away. "My father was a warrior. A hero," she said. "He would not want me to run from a challenge."

"Your father was indeed a hero," Jepson agreed. "When I served him in the war, I never saw a more wise or compassionate leader. He did his duty, but he did not hate his enemy—he did not allow that emotion to control him."

"My duty is to avenge my parents," she argued.

"Your duty is to break the spell so Morganna cannot continue to ruin the lives of other innocents," he replied.

She turned back to him. "But, she believes all the Herdins are dead. Surely, there is no need to continue her cruel campaign."

"Morganna has allowed anger and the thirst for retribution to change her," he said. "There is no logic in her actions, only a desire for more power and an appetite for cruelty that can only be satisfied with increasing malevolence."

"The villagers?" Meaghan asked. "Those under my father's protection?"

"What do you think, milady?" Jepson asked softly.

"But surely Monty…"

"Do you think she will allow Monty to stand in her way?" he asked. "His birth was a means to an end."

Her sigh came from the depths of her heart. "What must I do?" she asked.

"Let's go to the Old Mother and have her read your fortune," he suggested, referring to the matriarch of the gypsy camp. "She will be able to give you the direction you seek."

"Fortune telling?" Meaghan asked, shaking her head. "But that's not real."

Jepson chuckled softly. "You who have had green fairies touch your face and the Eochaidh protect you, you wonder about fortune telling?" he teased. "When will you learn that there is more to this life that we don't understand than what we do?"

Chapter Seventeen

The gypsies had closed off the camp to outsiders since the death of Lord and Lady Herdin. There were no shows, no bartering, and no games of chance. They had said it was as a sign of respect, but Meaghan knew it was also because they were protecting her and hiding her from those in the village who would kill her if they knew she was still alive.

With the shawl around her head and shoulders, she slowly walked with Jepson through the camp. Children chased each other, laughing and teasing, as they ran across the wet grass. Mothers washed clothing in kettles hanging over wood fires. Fathers sat together, smoking their pipes and looking out to the horizon, watching the weather.

Most of the wagons were huddled together near the top of the hill. The massive, sturdy, caravan horses were housed together in a makeshift paddock underneath the limbs of a giant, old oak tree. It was like a small, moveable village, the people working together in perfect harmony.

The ground beneath her feet was soggy, with puddles of mud covering much of the grass. Meaghan could feel the cold water enter her cloth shoes and squish between her toes. Walking slowly, aware of Jepson's limitations, she was able to study the other members of the caravan. She realized they never made eye contact with her, and when she approached, they would hurry to another area of the camp.

"They fear your magic," Jepson whispered, once again knowing Meaghan's thoughts before she had a chance to voice them.

"I have no magic," she said, turning towards him and catching him in an unguarded moment, the pain obvious on his face.

How he'd stayed on his feet during the past week was a mystery to her. But whenever she'd encouraged him to rest, he had obstinately denied having any pain. It was only when she would sit quietly that he would allow himself time to rest. She looked ahead. The wagon they sought was at the very farthest point of the camp.

"Why does her wagon have to be so far away?" Meaghan asked, concerned with Jepson's discomfort.

"The others protect her," Jepson replied.

"Because she is so old?" Meaghan asked.

Jepson shook his head. "Because she is so valuable," he said. "Her knowledge and her guidance have saved this gypsy family many times."

"Does she have magic?" she asked.

Jepson was silent for a few moments as they walked down a rocky, muddied dirt path toward the colorful wagon. "What is magic?" he finally asked.

She shook her head and even managed a soft chuckle. "Have I ever mentioned how frustrating it is to have someone answer a question with another question?" she asked.

He laughed softly. "I only do so because often the answer you hold within your mind is the best answer for your heart," he said.

She sighed and nodded. "What is magic?" she asked, repeating his question slowly.

Immediately, her mind went back to a week earlier when Lady Strathmore, no she reminded herself, Morganna created the storm that destroyed her home and killed everyone inside.

Then her thoughts went back further, to the secret glen where she hid from the magistrate's men who were trying to kill her. She pictured the long, sweeping branches of the willow trees that cascaded down into the clear, blue water and the fireflies that danced within the green curtains. She remembered the water sprites on the lily pads who jumped into the air and created their own unique dance above the placid waters.

Those memories brought to mind the tiny, green fairy who had approached Meaghan in the forest, playing and teasing until she flew away into the brush.

All of that was magic.

Then, unbidden, came the memory of her parents laughing with each other, the tender looks they would exchange when they thought no one else was watching, the unspoken communication they shared that was unique to those in love.

That was magic.

She finally turned to Jepson. "Magic is the power to take something ordinary and turn it into something extraordinary," she said.

"And which magic do you believe is the most powerful?" he asked.

She answered without reservation. "The kind that comes from within, from your heart," she replied.

He smiled at her and nodded. "You are ready to see the Old Mother now."

Chapter Eighteen

The elegant, black carriage careened down the muddy and slippery road, nearly running over several townspeople in its wake. The horses, foaming at the mouth and exhausted, struggled to pull the heavy vehicle up the steep hill to what was left of the Dunower estate.

"Go faster," Lady Strathmore called from the plush insides of the carriage as she beat with her parasol against the small hatch on the roof.

The hatch slid open, and one of her footmen peered in. "We've got 'em full out, milady," he said. "We can't push them any harder or we'll kill 'em."

"Are there not sufficient horses at the Dunower stable to replace them should they die?" she asked angrily. "Whip them!"

She heard the crack of the whip and smiled with satisfaction. Nothing—not man or beast—would stand in her way.

The carriage finally pulled to a stop in front of the ruins of the estate. Herdin grooms ran forward to rescue the horses who were struggling to breathe and remain standing. Lady Strathmore pushed open the carriage door. "You, there," she cried, pointing at the nearest groom. "See to my horses immediately. And if they are harmed, it will be on your head."

The groom rushed forward to unhitch the heaving mounts and slowly guide them away from the carriage.

"Mother, what are you doing here?" Lord Montgomery Strathmore, the new Eleventh Earl of Dunower, strode across the muddy ground toward the carriage.

Allowing the footmen to help her down, she smiled at her son as she lifted her skirts slightly so they wouldn't touch the muddy ground. "I remembered that Meaghan had a lovely, spirited mare, and I've decided that I would like to have her as my own," she called casually.

Monty's face paled, and he glanced over at the remaining staff of the Herdin household, wondering if they'd overheard. He hurried over to stand in front of her. "Mother," he said, his voice low. "Her body is barely cold. I do not think it's respectable for us to be distributing her belongings."

"That's nonsense," Lady Strathmore replied. "She obviously has no use for her horse now and I do."

She turned and saw one of the Herdin family grooms. "You!" she called. "Bring Lady Meaghan's horse to me."

"Mother, no," Monty said. "No. You cannot take Meggie's horse."

"Of course I can," Lady Strathmore said. "Until you marry, I am the Countess Dunower." She patted his shoulder and shook her head. "Really, Monty, you need to understand your position. As the new Earl of Dunower, you cannot allow trivial, emotional sentiments to blind you to your duties."

"Mother, I said no," he repeated angrily.

Lady Strathmore stared back at her son. "Do not take that tone with me," she warned. "I have allowed you to traipse about our home with your maudlin expressions of grief. I have allowed you to mingle with the most common element of our village as you work to restore our new home. But on this, Monty, you have no say. I will have Lady Meaghan's mount."

"Begging your pardon, milord," a groom interrupted. "But Lady Meaghan's mount ain't in the stables."

"What?" Lady Strathmore exclaimed. "Don't lie to me."

She walked over to the front of the carriage and picked up the whip. With a swing of her arm, she snapped the whip in the air and then walked toward the frightened groom. "Now, you will tell me the truth," she screamed, lifting her arm into the air once more.

Monty grabbed her arm and pulled the whip out of her hand. "Mother, stop," he demanded. "The groom is quite right. As I recall, we were not able to find Meggie's horse to pull her hearse. She must have bolted the night of the fire."

Lady Strathmore's eyes widened with concern. "Did any of the other horses bolt?" she asked.

The groom shook his head. "But, it could be that Lady Meaghan's horse was not in her stall," he said. "She went out on her horse late that afternoon. I helped her myself."

"Do you remember when she came back?" Lady Strathmore asked softly, but the tone of her voice caused a chill to run down the groom's back.

He swallowed and shook his head. "No, your ladyship," he said. "But with the fire and all...everything was so confusing..."

She turned from the groom to her son. "Monty, you need to send some of your men up to the gypsy camp," she said. "I have no doubt that they have stolen Meaghan's horse and probably several others. I don't know why you have allowed them to stay."

"Because Lord Herdin allowed them to stay," Monty said with a tired sigh.

"But he is dead," she responded tightly. "And he no longer has a say in these matters."

She turned back to the groom. "I need new horses for my carriage," she demanded. "Get them now!"

Then she turned to Monty. "If you won't investigate the gypsy camp," she said, "I will."

Chapter Nineteen

Jepson leaned forward and knocked on the door of the ornate, gypsy wagon that was nestled amidst a small grove of trees. The wagon creaked and shifted slightly as there was movement within its brightly colored walls. Finally, the door creaked opened, and Meaghan saw the Old Mother standing in the doorway, her dark eyes curiously taking in the scene before her.

She nodded to Meaghan. "You wish to know your future?" she asked.

Meaghan shrugged slightly. "I wish to know what I should do," she replied.

The old woman smiled widely, showing her yellowed teeth, and nodded. "This good," she said. "This very good and not too soon." She looked beyond them and out to the horizon. "We must hurry. Come! Come in now."

Meaghan hurried forward and climbed up the rickety steps that led to the door. Old Mother stepped aside so she could enter. Then Jepson started up, and Old Mother held out her hand, stopping him.

"This knowledge for the lady only," she said, lowering her voice so only he could hear her. "Gather her things together, quickly. There is danger in the air."

With no argument, Jepson turned and hurried back toward the main camp. Old Mother watched him walk away and nodded in approval. She glanced once again towards the horizon and slowly shook her head. "Is not good," she whispered. Then she closed the door and turned towards Meaghan.

The interior of the wagon was more colorful than the exterior. Bright color fabrics hung from the ceiling to separate the sleeping quarters from the living quarters. Pots, pans, knickknacks and clothing hung from small hooks all around the exterior of the room. A small cot covered with brightly patterned pillows was tucked in one corner. A white porcelain basin lay on the floor next to it, and small packets of various herbs lay in the basin.

In the center of the wagon was a small, round table covered with a silk material in a dark paisley pattern. There were two chairs on either side of the table, and Old Mother pointed to one.

"You sit," she said, and Meaghan immediately obeyed.

The old woman sat across from her and sat quietly for a long moment, her dark, almost birdlike, eyes studying the young woman in front of her. Finally, she nodded. "I see your hands?" she asked.

Meaghan held her hands out, trying to keep them from trembling.

The old woman looked from Meaghan's hands to her eyes. "You are afraid, yes?"

Meaghan nodded. "Yes," she whispered, her throat dry.

"Is good to be afraid," the old woman said. "Is bad to be a coward."

"I'm not a coward," Meaghan said.

The woman smiled slowly and nodded. Then she took Meaghan's hands in her own, and Meaghan shuddered at her touch. But Old Mother did not look up. She kept her eyes down, studying the small, delicate hands that lay in her tough, hardened, old ones.

"You must be brave," Old Mother whispered, "for the task before you is great. There is evil—old, powerful evil that wishes to stop you."

"Morganna," Meaghan whispered.

Old Mother nodded. "Yes, and those who do her bidding," she said. "You have a quest before you." She paused for a long moment. "And you must seek out those whose lives have been entwined with your own."

She looked up and met Meaghan's eyes. "You must trust," she said.

Meaghan shook her head. "No, they lied to me," she argued. "They caused my parents' death."

"Your path is connected," Old Mother continued, turning her gaze back to Meaghan's hands. "Without them, no success for you. Without you, death for them."

"Death?" Meaghan exclaimed. "They would be killed? What must I do?"

"You must complete quest. You must break spell," the old woman replied.

"But she is so strong," Meaghan said, her voice catching. "How can I fight her?"

"You are stronger than she. You must believe," Old Mother said.

"But she has so much power," Meaghan replied. "She can create storms and bolts of lightning. How do I fight that?"

Old Mother's eyes glazed over, and her voice deepened. "In an ancient forest, there is an old quarry where, in ancient times, men mined for jewels for their kings and queens. The quarry also held great temptation for those who knew the power of the gems, and so it was often raided and the miners left for dead. Merlin, who had a great fondness for the gems, decided to use his power to protect the miners. As a solution, Merlin took one of the gemstones, a moon opal, and set a spell upon it. The spell protected those who possessed the gem against the powers of darkness."

"How do I find it?" Meaghan asked. "Where is the quarry?"

Old Mother looked up, her eyes wide and her voice suddenly urgent. "You must go now," she urged. "You must go alone. You must go to the forest and find them. They will help you find the gem."

Meaghan's heart pounded in her chest. "Now?" she asked. "But I'm not ready."

"Go now, or all is lost," Old Mother said.

Meaghan jumped up and hurried to the door. She pulled it open just as Jepson was hurrying towards her with her horse and pack.

"Someone is coming from the village," he said. "It looks like the Strathmore carriage."

"Morganna," Meaghan whispered, her heart in her throat.

"We must—" Jepson began.

"No," Old Mother said from behind Meaghan. "She must go alone. You must stay. She must leave now."

Jepson helped Meaghan onto her horse. "I promised your father…" he began.

Meaghan leaned over and placed her hand on Jepson's shoulder. "Help Monty," Meaghan said. "Morganna will try to destroy him."

Jepson nodded and stepped away from her. "God speed, Lady Meaghan," he whispered. "Now go. Quickly."

He slapped the horse's haunches, and it bolted away from the camp and towards the old woods.

"Will she be safe?" Jepson asked Old Mother.

"She must be," she replied. "She is our only hope."

Chapter Twenty

Meaghan leaned forward on her horse, urging it forward. The narrow path that skirted down the back of the hill was steep and slippery, but both rider and horse felt the urgency to move as quickly as possible. Her heart was pounding in her chest, and her mind was reeling from her time with Old Mother. She wasn't ready. She wasn't prepared. How could she even consider leaving everything and everyone and venture out on her own?

She wasn't a warrior.

She was terrified.

Reaching the base of the hill, Meaghan pulled her horse to a halt and looked across the meadow to the old forest, about a quarter of a mile away. There was no way to cross it without being seen. Even if she tried to skirt the meadow, the road alongside it was just as exposed.

Impatiently, her horse pawed at the ground, and Meaghan felt the thrum of danger in her heart too. She could hear loud voices from above them on the hill, and knew she was wasting crucial moments as she hesitated there. Finally, with an air of resignation, she took a deep breath and urged her horse forward through the middle of the meadow.

She leaned forward, her body horizontal with her horse, and gave her horse free rein. The horse galloped forward, the meadow passing beneath them as a blur.

Suddenly the sky burst above them, and sheets of rain poured down, soaking them.

"Really?" Meaghan exclaimed as rivulets of water poured down her face. Then she glanced around and realized the dark rain clouds had blocked the sun and provided them with a cover nearly like nightfall. She looked up to the sky, water splashing against her face, and laughed.

"Thank you," she said, as darkness settled around them. "Thank you!"

Suddenly, a large, white owl appeared and soared silently in the darkened sky. It dove towards her and, panicked, she kicked the stirrups. Her horse lunged forward, and they sped together towards the safety of the old forest. The owl hovered above her for a few yards then turned and flew back in the direction of the gypsy camp.

Meaghan breathed a sigh of relief, both from the departure of the owl and the entrance of the old forest only a few yards ahead. She leaned forward, encouraging her horse to maintain its speed until they were within the shelter of the trees. Finally, when Meaghan felt she could no longer be seen by anyone looking from the hill, she pulled her horse to a stop.

The thick canopy of trees prevented most of the rain from hitting the ground. Only the wind rustling the leaves brought a lighter shower of gentle raindrops. Taking a deep breath, Meaghan looked ahead of her into the darkness of the woods. She patted her horse's neck, more to reassure herself than the horse.

"It's fine," she whispered. "We've been here before. There's nothing to be afraid of."

The horse nickered softly in response and then pawed at the soft dirt of the path.

"Yes, you're right," Meaghan replied taking a deep breath. "We should move on."

She lightly slapped the reins, and her horse stepped forward toward the dark path ahead. Suddenly, the trees were lit by the glow of thousands of fireflies, creating a warm and welcoming path into the old forest.

Meaghan smiled. "Okay, now we can really go," she said.

She urged her horse on, and they galloped forward into the depths of the woods.

Chapter Twenty-one

The black carriage rocked back and forth as it was pulled up the dirt path to the top of the hill where the gypsy camp lay. But the carriage itself was not what was worrying Jepson as he made his way toward the front of the camp. It was the dozen horses and riders that followed it. He recognized the men as the ones who had come into the camp more than a week ago, under the direction of the magistrate, and arrested him under false pretenses.

"This is evil," Old Mother said to him as they neared the entrance to the camp.

Jepson put a hand on her shoulder. "You should stay here," he said, "where it is safe."

She shook her head. "When people hide from evil, there is no safety," she replied. "I will come with you."

The men in the camp had gathered together with whatever weapons they could find and stood in a circle blocking the entrance. The carriage barreled forward and slid to a stop just inches from the men.

The magistrate's men dismounted and walked over to stand beside the carriage. They carried swords and clubs, but some carried flaming torches.

"Let's burn it down," one of the men cried out, and the others answered in a cheering roar.

Slamming the carriage door open, Lady Strathmore stepped down from the carriage, a whip in her hand. Her men quieted immediately. "We will act appropriately," she said to them, a knowing smile on her lips. "But if we are merely defending ourselves, then we must do what we must do."

She turned to the gypsies. "I will take my property," she demanded, cracking the whip in the air. "And I will take it now."

"And what is the property of which you speak?" asked an ageing voice from behind the line of men. Suddenly, the men parted, and Old Mother walked slowly forward to meet Lady Strathmore.

"You are in charge of these thieves and thugs, I presume?" Lady Strathmore spat.

Old Mother stood quietly for a moment, studying the woman before her. "You are not as you would lead us to believe," she said softly.

"I do not care what you believe," Lady Strathmore countered. "I will have my property."

Old Mother nodded. "And I ask you again, what is the property of which you speak?"

"My horse," Lady Strathmore countered. "A chestnut mare, about fourteen hands tall with four white stockings."

"And this is your horse?" Old Mother asked.

"It is now," Lady Strathmore hissed. "And whoever stole her will be hung for horse theft."

"You mistake," Old Mother replied. "We do not have this animal. It was the horse of Lady Meaghan, no?"

Lady Strathmore seethed and tightened her grip on the whip. "It was, yes," she replied, stepping up closer to Old Mother. "But now it is mine."

Old Mother lifted her head and met Lady Strathmore's eyes. "What you seek is not here," she said firmly.

Lady Strathmore slapped the old woman hard enough that Old Mother stumbled back a few steps. Immediately, Jepson was there, catching her so she wouldn't fall and steadying her on her feet. "Old Mother," he whispered.

The old woman rubbed the red mark on her skin, and her eyes welled with tears. She took a deep breath. "Do not let her provoke us into a fight," she whispered.

Jepson nodded. "Yes, Old Mother," he agreed.

He nodded to several of the gypsy women, and they hurried forward to encircle the old woman. Then he turned and stepped up to face Lady Strathmore.

"I know you," Lady Strathmore said. "You're one of the Herdin stable dogs. Did you run away from the fire to save yourself?"

"This camp is closed to visitors," he said softly, his jaw clenched in rage.

"You are the visitors," Lady Strathmore argued. "And you are welcome no longer. You are to leave my property immediately."

"This is not your property," Jepson replied.

"Herdin is dead," she spat. "My son is now Lord of this land. You will leave now."

"We will leave when your son asks us to leave," Jepson replied.

"My son and I are of one mind in these matters," she exclaimed.

Jepson folded his arms across his chest and stared boldly at the woman before him. "Your son will honor the agreement Lord Herdin made with the gypsies. He is a man of integrity."

Lady Strathmore's eyes narrowed. "Do you dare disparage my character?" she snarled. She looked over her shoulder to the two large, brutish men who stood behind her. "This one needs a lesson on manners. Hold him."

The two men rushed forward and grabbed Jepson before he could move. They roughly pulled him forward, tormenting his broken ribs, and then stopped next to her carriage.

"Tie him to the side of the carriage," she directed.

The men lashed Jepson to the wagon and then tore his shirt off his back, exposing the bruises and welts from his encounter with the magistrate.

The gypsies began to move forward, brandishing their knives and simple weapons.

"No," Jepson called to them, fearing worse retribution from the other angry men that stood just beyond the carriage. "Do not fight them. I will be fine."

"Do you think so?" Lady Strathmore said, stepping back behind Jepson and lifting her whip over her head. "I suppose we will see."

She moved her arm back to add power to the slash of the whip and then brought it forward with wicked bliss. But before she could complete the lashing, something clamped on her wrist, and her arm was stayed.

She turned in anger. "Who dare…" she screamed, and then her words sputtered to a stop.

"My lady," the older gentleman said slowly, capturing her gaze in his own. "How fortuitous it is that we meet, once again."

"You cannot be here," she whispered, stunned and afraid.

"And yet, I am," he replied calmly.

She took a deep breath and then pulled her hand from his grasp. "You have lost," she said, a malicious smile in her eyes. "You have lost it all."

He shrugged easily. "As you say," he replied.

She studied him intently and then turned and looked at Jepson, understanding blossoming on her face. "She did not die," she whispered, her face filled with rage.

Chapter Twenty-two

Jepson rubbed his wrists with the salve Old Mother gave him as he walked to the edge of the camp with the man who had saved him from a beating. "I do not understand, Fitz. How did you escape the fire?" he finally asked when they were far enough away from the others.

"I happened to be outside, waiting for you and Lady Meaghan to arrive," Fitz replied easily. "The explosion blew me backwards, away from the house. I must have hit my head, for I have no memory of the past few days."

Jepson studied the tall man beside him and then shook his head. "I will not ask you more than you are willing to tell me," he said. "But I do not welcome lies."

The butler was silent for a moment. "I should be quite offended by that comment," he finally replied.

Jepson shrugged. "And I should be offended that you would think I would accept such a falsehood."

A smirk played over the butler's lips, and he nodded. "Indeed," he replied. "Indeed."

He folded his arms over his chest and cocked his head to the side. "And if what I said is a falsehood, what is the answer to your question?"

Jepson looked over his shoulder to ensure they were truly alone and then nodded. "There is only one who can put fear into the face of Morganna," he whispered.

"You know that she is Morganna?" Fitz asked, shocked.

"We saw her, Lady Meaghan and I, cast the spell and bring down the lightning bolt," Jepson replied. "Lady Meaghan wanted to stop her, but one of the Eochaidh held her back."

"Probably saved her life," Fitz murmured.

Jepson nodded. "I agree," he said. "But she was not grateful. She would have willingly died to stop Morganna."

"And Morganna would have willingly killed her," Fitz replied.

"And so, Master Wizard, Merlin the Powerful, what can we do to stop Morganna?"

Fitz raised one hoary eyebrow and studied Jepson. "You presume much."

Jepson glanced around again and then stepped closer to Fitz. "Lady Meaghan left only moments before Morganna and her underlings approached the camp," he whispered. "Old Mother read her fortune and sent her off."

Fitz nodded. "Yes, I saw her riding toward the forest, and I hurried her on her way."

"You saw her?" Jepson asked, confused. "So, she knows that her butler and Merlin are one?"

Fitz shook his head. "No, that is only a puzzle her astute companion has realized," he said. "She only saw a large snowy owl, that's all."

"I will get some horses," Jepson said eagerly. "If we hurry, we can overtake her by nightfall."

He started to move, but Fitz put a hand on his shoulder to stop him. Jepson looked up at Fitz. "What? Why do you stop me?"

"We cannot accompany her on this quest," Fitz said, shaking his head sadly. "It is for her to accomplish alone."

"But it's dangerous. She could die," Jepson exclaimed, anger and frustration building inside him. "If you are too afraid, you can stay. But I am going to help her."

"You forget yourself, gypsy," Fitz replied angrily. Then his voice softened. "But I admire your fealty to Lady Meaghan and to the promise you made to her father. But you also understand the ways of magic. Would you risk her life because you did not trust her strength?"

Tears of frustration filled Jepson's eyes, and he brushed them away impatiently. "What would you have me do?" he asked, his voice hoarse with despair.

"What did Lady Meaghan ask of you?" Fitz asked.

Jepson sighed. "She asked me to help Monty," he answered reluctantly.

Fitz nodded slowly and looked past Jepson, across the valley to where the ruins of the estate lay. "I do not believe the young man realizes the power of his birthright," Fitz said. "He might be able to use your help to understand who he is."

"The new Earl of Dunower?" Jepson asked bitterly.

Fitz looked back to Jepson and shook his head. "No, the son of Morganna," he said easily. "The son of a sorceress."

Chapter Twenty-three

With the meadow securely behind her and the forest now encircling her, Meaghan slowed her horse's pace to a walk. She came to a fork in the path and stopped. Both of the trails were rugged and unused, with brush nearly taking them over. With the sun hidden in the clouds, she couldn't be sure which path would take her in the right direction, toward the hidden grove.

Suddenly, the path on the right lit up with the tiny lights from the fireflies, and Meaghan realized they weren't just illuminating her way they were guiding her to where she needed to go. With no hesitation, she loosened the reins and guided her horse down the right path, toward her duty.

The clop of her horse's hooves against the hard dirt echoed in the woods, contrasting with the soft sounds of birds singing, leaves rustling and a river babbling in the distance—sounds that still brought her comfort and a feeling of home. As she moved forward, things began to look more familiar.

She had traveled some of these paths before. She had explored them with her father.

Suddenly, the dense foliage opened to expose the banks of the river she'd heard earlier. She dismounted and led her horse to the water to drink. Stretching, she gazed at the trees around her and the bank on the other side of the rushing, clear waters. Then it came to her. This was the place where only ten days ago she and her father had met. This was where she'd tumbled him into the brook. This was where, in a moment of pure fun, he'd pulled a brook trout from his shirt.

The memory was so clear.

And once it drifted away, her loss was intensified.

Grief, powerful and all-encompassing, racked her body. She slowly dropped to the ground, and the pain inside demanded release. Bending over, curled up in a ball, she moaned softly, and then her shoulders shook with despair. Tears filled her eyes and streamed down her face as she wept for her loss, wept for the sweet voices she would never hear again, wept for the new memories that would never be made, wept for a future that had been torn from her fingers. And she wept knowing that she never got to say goodbye.

The heartache poured from her until she was gasping for breath and exhausted from her tears. She took a quick, shuddering breath and sat up, wiping the tears from her face with her rough shawl. She slowly took another breath, and the shuddering lessened. Finally, her hand on her stirrups to help her, she pulled herself up onto her feet and leaned against her horse.

"I need to say goodbye," she whispered, and her horse, as if she understood, nickered softly.

Looking around, Meaghan spied a patch of heather growing close by. She hurried and gathered some together. Then she found a patch of wood anemones, a bright, buttercup-like flower that her father had said made him happy just looking at them. Picking a small bouquet of the petite flowers, she added them to the handful of heather and walked back to the river's edge.

Alongside the river was a fallen silver birch tree, its light bark falling off the trunk. Meaghan picked up a square piece of the bark that was six inches across and placed the small bouquet on it and walked back to her horse. She knelt at the water's edge, the small raft with its fragrant passengers in her hands.

"Silver birch for renewal and for love," she whispered, her voice breaking. "Heather for you, mother. And anemones for you, father. My only comfort is that you are still together. I miss you. I miss you so much my heart hurts."

She took a deep breath and released it slowly.

"I will do my duty," she vowed. "I will uphold the Herdin legacy. I will beat Morganna and stop her from destroying any more lives."

She placed the raft into the flowing waters and watched it as it slowly drifted away. "Goodbye," she wept softly, rubbing away her tears. "I love you."

Finally, she stood and watched the river until the small raft had drifted out of sight. With a final sigh, she mounted her horse and then patted her horse's neck. "Let's go," she whispered, and they continued down the path that was lit by the fireflies.

A few minutes after Meaghan had left the riverbank, two large, dark shadows stepped out from a grove of trees on the other side.

"She would not have been happy to know we witnessed her grief," Rufus said.

Tristan nodded. "Aye, but for her protection, we needed to stay," he replied.

Rufus shook his head. "No, lad, she was safe enough," he said. "Admit it. It was like watching a sacred ceremony. Her love for her parents is a wondrous thing."

"And her sorrow is so strong you can feel it," Tristan agreed. "Do we ask too much of her?"

"We don't ask it," Rufus said. "Whatever portion of fate intertwined the Herdin family with our curse asks it of her. And without her, we are doomed."

Chapter Twenty-four

The old yew was hidden behind the stables in the courtyard of the Brigid's Well Inn. The downpour had halted any traffic, and the black carriage was able to travel through the courtyard and back behind the stables unseen. Morganna, dressed as Lady Strathmore, slipped from the interior of the carriage, stepped up next to the trunk of the old tree, clasped her amulet in her bare hand and whispered the words of the spell.

Once again, she watched through the branches of the tree as day became night, as days blurred together, then years, decades and centuries. The movement stopped abruptly. The yew was only a sapling, and she stepped back onto a wholly different landscape. The landscape of Camelot of old.

That her carriage was waiting for her was not an accident. She had ordered her men to remain there, awaiting her arrival however long that took. Her henchmen immediately jumped to attention, opening the door to her carriage and assisting her into the small space.

"Take me to my castle," she ordered. "Quickly."

When they arrived at the beginning of the narrow isthmus that led to the island, the tide had already covered the sandy path to her castle. The driver only hesitated a moment then cracked the whip over the heads of the horses, sending them plunging forward into the sea water. Spray arched up over the carriage wheels, and the driver fought the reins to keep the horses on the narrow, sandy path. The horses splashed through the waves that were lapping up to their forelocks but finally pulled the carriage to a stop in front of the stone fortress.

Morganna forcefully pushed the door of the carriage open so it slammed against the carriage's frame. "Why is no one here to help me out?" she screamed, and a young footman jumped from the top of the carriage to quickly assist her.

After stepping down, she shoved the young man out of her way and hurried forward into the cool darkness of her castle. She dropped her cloak on the stairs behind her and rushed into her potion room.

Rushing to one of the counters, she located a small vial that held a miniscule amount of blood in it.

She turned and smiled at the rotting corpse lying in the corner of the room, lifting the vial in a toast. "Well, done, Sir Magistrate," she whispered. "You actually served me well."

With a swish of her skirts, she turned and hurried up the narrow stairs that led to the small tower room. She hurried across the pentagram on the floor and stood over the silver bowl. As she had done before, she dripped a drop of blood into the clear water in the bowl.

Instantly, the water began to foam, and a gray mist bubbled over the sides of the bowl, pouring onto the floor.

"Show me," she commanded. She lifted her hands towards the skies and threw back her head. She whispered the words of the spell she'd used before and, once again, the room darkened, and the wind swirled around her.

When she could finally see a picture in the water, she studied it carefully and screamed in anger.

"How can this be?" she shouted, her voice echoing off the walls. "She should be dead!"

She took a deep breath to calm herself and then watched as Meaghan set the small piece of bark laden with flowers into the river.

"How sweet," Morganna sneered sarcastically. "Farewell to a bothersome couple if there ever was one."

She watched as Meaghan mounted her horse and continued down the path.

She stepped away from the bowl just before Tristan and Rufus appeared in the water. She walked to one of the windows in the tower. "The girl must die," she seethed, "before she finds the knights."

She turned back and looked into the bowl. The scene before her was a deserted riverbank with birds singing in the distance. She lifted her hand to strike the bowl and send it sailing across the room but then thought better of it and released a frustrated sigh.

"Control yourself, Morganna," she whispered, lowering her arm. "You only have so much blood to see into the future. You mustn't waste it."

She looked back into the bowl. "Don't be sad, Lady Meaghan," she called into the water. "Soon you will be joining your dear parents."

Chapter Twenty-five

Meaghan shivered as a cold wind traveled up the path and seemed to swirl around her before it continued on. She pulled her shawl closer and pulled her horse to a stop. Were those words she heard in the wind? She shivered again. That wind had an ominous feeling to it.

She urged her horse forward again toward the hidden grove. Would Tristan still be there? Had the Eochaidh moved on when she walked away from Tristan the night her parents died?

She could still feel the anger and the hurt from their last meeting and tried to examine her feelings. Were they justified?

She had come to the woods to meet with him because he told her he could show her the Eochaidh. She wanted to meet them and get their help to protect her family from Morganna. But he hadn't told her that he was Eochaidh, he hadn't planned on bringing her to the other enchanted knights. And, while she was with him, wasting her time, her parents and her entire household were murdered by Morganna's magic.

She sighed softly and she had to admit that he wasn't all bad. He had rescued her, twice—once from the magistrate's men when they were trying to kill her and stop her family from ending the curse, and then once when she had tumbled down the side of the ravine. Both times, if he hadn't come, she could have been killed. He had risked his own safety, especially if they thought Morganna was near, in order to save her.

She nodded to herself. Maybe there was a good reason for him not to tell her who he was. Maybe he didn't know if he could trust her.

Once again, reason made her consider that, given time, he would have told her that he was one of the Eochaidh. And, even if he had agreed to help, what could they have done to counteract Morganna's spell?

"Well, I guess we'll never know," she said aloud with more than a little impertinence.

"We'll never know what?"

Meaghan gasped and then breathed a sigh of relief when Tristan stepped out of the forest onto the path. Then her heart betrayed her and fluttered at the sight of him.

When she first met Tristan, she immediately realized he was no local farmer or farmer's son. His voice was too refined, his manners too polished, and his motives, for the most part, were to aid and protect. Although, he was no nobleman's son either. He was too muscled, like the blacksmith, but not as bulky, more like one of her father's thoroughbreds with lean, long lines.

He spoke with authority and leadership; Meaghan knew he was no one's servant. His face, although young, was also strong and well-formed. His eyes were as she remembered, an amazing shade of blue. But this time, his eyes held her own with a look of regret.

"I didn't mean to startle you," he said softly.

She shook her head. "It was my own fault," she admitted. "I was lost in my thoughts. I should have been more aware."

He came up next to her, standing near the neck of her horse. "And what will we never know?" he asked again.

She looked down at him and decided to start this quest with honesty. "We will never know if you had chosen to tell me the truth, if that would have made a difference," she said. "If somehow we could have saved my parents."

His eyes were bleak for a moment, and Meaghan could see real regret. Then he nodded. "You're right. We will never know," he agreed softly. "And I beg your pardon for not telling you the truth."

"It was not his truth to tell," added Rufus as he too stepped forward from the brush. "He brought it to a vote. He wanted to tell you, but the rest of us chose to wait until we knew more about you, lass."

"More about me?" Meaghan asked the large, red-headed man.

"Aye, there are many who are in league with Morganna," he replied.

She nodded. "Like the magistrate and his men."

"And it's not easy to tell foe from friend," he continued. "At least not at first."

"And was I such a threat?" she asked.

Rufus smiled at her. "I've watched you here in the forest with your father, lassie," he said. "You've the heart of a lion."

Meaghan's eyes filled with tears, and she brushed them away quickly. "Thank you for your honesty," she replied quietly.

"Come," Tristan said quickly, hating the pain he saw in her eyes. "Let's get you to our camp so you can meet the others."

Meaghan was startled even more when both men suddenly turned into massive horses and made their way down the narrow path, one in front of her and one behind. "So, the legend is true," she exclaimed.

"Aye, lass," Rufus replied from behind her. "And the danger is real."

Chapter Twenty-six

As Meaghan followed Tristan's lead, she was surprised when he left the main and followed a very narrow, almost indistinguishable trail deeper into the woods.

"I don't believe I've been on this path before," she said, looking over her shoulder to Rufus.

"It's one of the paths we've used here for years," he explained. "But we're careful to not overuse any path. We don't want anyone tracking us."

"Are we going to the hidden grove?" she asked.

He nodded his big head, his red mane shaking in response. "Aye, the one you found on your own," he replied. "You've a rare way with the fae."

She shrugged dismissively. "It's nothing."

"Lass, I've lived for over a thousand years now," he said. "And I've never seen the likes of a green fairy allowing herself to be seen, much less touched, by a human. It's rare indeed."

Their conversation was interrupted when Tristan turned right into a thicket on the side of the trail. Meaghan rode up to it and stopped. The branches were so close together they were like a wall. How did he get through? And, more to the point, how was she supposed to get through?

"Sometimes, lass, you have to take the first step before the magic can happen," Rufus advised softly.

Taking a deep breath, Meaghan clicked to her horse to go forward, and once they stepped off the path, the branches opened before them, revealing a more worn path that led to the grove.

"How?" Meaghan asked.

"The wee fairies think it a game to let us in and out of their domain," he said. "They also guard the entrance so those who would do us harm cannot enter."

Looking back over her shoulder as the branches closed solidly behind Rufus, her eyes rounded in amazement. "That is truly magical."

He nodded. "Aye, it is."

A few moments later, Meaghan entered the grove. Tristan led her to the center. Then he and Rufus turned back to men. Tristan walked over to her.

"Allow me to help you dismount," he said. She leaned towards him, and he placed his hands around her waist and lifted her down from the saddle. Once again, she felt the traitorous fluttering of her heart. He placed her on the ground, and his hands lingered for just a moment longer than needed. Meaghan felt the blood rush to her face, and she quickly stepped back and away from him.

"Will you not introduce the rest of us to Lady Meaghan?" another male voice asked.

Meaghan turned around quickly, surprised to see three more knights standing before her.

"These are my compatriots," Tristan explained. "Sir Garrett, Sir Duncan and Sir Andrew."

At the mention of their names, each knight bowed slightly, and Meaghan curtsied in return.

"We are honored that you decided to join us," Duncan said.

Meaghan shook her head. "I would not have come if the Old Mother had not persuaded me that my duty lies in helping you break the spell."

"I am still not convinced that a mere lass can help us break it," Garrett said insolently. "All this might be for naught."

Meaghan turned to him, her eyes narrowed in anger. "Well, what choice do you have?" she snapped. "As you were too afraid to help save the life of the only male Herdin."

Garrett smiled slightly. "The kitten has claws."

"And a sword and a knife," Meaghan replied.

"If we are to reach the castle ruins by the solstice, we must travel quickly," Duncan said, "and start at first light." He looked at Meaghan. "Are you willing to do that?"

Meaghan nodded. "Yes, but the Old Mother told me of an amulet, an opal, that I should retrieve in order to be protected by Morganna's spells. She said it was in a quarry that Merlin favored."

"I know of the place," Rufus said. "It's a little out of the way, but the trip would only delay us a half day."

"A half day is crucial at a time like this," Duncan argued. "And the roads to the quarry are well used. It would be difficult and time consuming to have to hide every time someone came upon us."

"Can you not travel as men?" Meaghan asked.

"We would have to travel for several days as men," Tristan said. "And we would age several decades. We would not be able to withstand the rigors of the journey."

Meaghan examined Tristan's face and realized he had gray hair at his temple and deeper lines on his face.

"You have aged because you came to my aid?" she asked.

He shrugged. "It was nothing," he said. "Mere years."

"How long a journey if we travel straight to the ruins?" she asked.

"Two days," Duncan said. "Which will give us time to prepare things for the spell."

She nodded slowly and turned back to Tristan. "Morganna believes me dead," she said. "I am in no danger. We can bypass the trip to the quarry and go directly to the castle ruins."

Chapter Twenty-seven

Jepson and Fitz rode down from the gypsy camp to the burnt remains of the Herdin estate. There was a work crew from the village going through the rubble, salvaging whatever they could and taking the rest to a large pile behind the stables.

They slowed their horses to a walk and observed the workers carefully. Finally, Fitz patted Jepson's arm. "There," he said softly. "In the remains of the study."

There, dressed in shirt sleeves and hunting pants, Monty was sifting through the piles of debris. His arms, torso and face were covered with soot. His hair was in disarray, and his boots were ruined.

The two men dismounted, tied their horses to a nearby sapling and walked slowly across the ground to the estate. Stepping carefully over downed timbers and plaster wall, they made their way through what had been the hallway to the study and walked up behind the young man.

Monty kicked aside a piece of charred wood panel and had started to bend over to the items underneath when he heard the footsteps behind him. He turned quickly. "May I help…" but his words died in his throat.

"Fitz?" he stammered. "Jepson? You're alive?"

He threw himself into the arms of the austere butler and sobbed. Fitz, uncomfortable with this show of emotion, froze for a moment and then, with a sigh, wrapped his arms around the young man. "Yes, we are alive," he said softly. "And we are here to serve you. You are the new…"

Monty raised his head, the tracks of his tears drawing lines in the soot. "Please, I beg of you," he whispered hoarsely. "Don't say that. I would give anything not to have the cursed title." His voice broke. "I would give anything to have the Herdin family… Meggie…"

He took an unsteady breath and then stepped away from Fitz, pulling his handkerchief out of his pocket and wiping his face. "I must apologize," he stammered. "I had no right…I realize that you too…"

He took a deep breath. "This is not easy for any of us."

Jepson stepped up and placed his hand on the young man's shoulder. "Lord John thought very highly of you," he said. "And he knew that you would always do the right thing."

Monty dropped his head for a moment and stared at the debris on the floor. Finally, he raised his head and met the eyes of the two men. "I don't know if I can do the right thing," he said sadly.

"You don't know?" Fitz asked, cocking his head to the side. "If you don't know, who would?"

"You don't understand," Monty explained. "My mother…Lady Strathmore…has ideas and protocols and plans…"

"And yet you are the Earl. She is not," Fitz replied softly.

Monty shook his head. "But don't I owe her some loyalty?" he asked. "She is, after all, my mother."

"What does your heart tell you?" Fitz asked. "What does it say to you in the quiet of the night?"

Monty paused and then carefully looked around. The other workers were far enough away that this conversation was still private. Yet, he still lowered his voice. "My heart tells me that something is amiss," he said softly. "If you must know the truth, my heart balks at the way she treats others, at her disregard for basic human kindness, at her lack of compassion."

"What do you know about your mother?" Fitz asked.

Shrugging, Monty pushed his hair off his forehead and took a deep breath. "I know that she did not love my father," he said. "And she had even less love for the Herdin family. I know that her great desire was for me to become Earl and for her to gain more power."

"Do you believe that the power of your new position is enough for her?" Jepson asked.

"No," Monty replied, shaking his head. "No, I can already see that her thirst for power will not be quenched here."

"It cannot be quenched here," Fitz explained. "Because she is not merely Lady Strathmore."

"What?" Monty asked. "What do you mean?"

Fitz paused for a moment and studied the young man before him, saw the confusion in his eyes but also the acknowledgement of truth. "Tell me, what do you know about Morganna?"

Chapter Twenty-eight

The setting sun cast a blood red hue over Arthur's castle and the entire city of Camelot. Morganna watched from a window in her chambers as the sun lowered, and soon the scene before lay in quiet twilight. She pushed herself away from the stone windowsill and walked across the room to the narrow staircase.

"Well, Lady Meaghan," she mused, "why don't we just see where your travels this day have led you."

She slowly walked up the stairs, the hem of her long dress sliding up the staircase behind her. When she reached the tower room, she went directly to the silver bowl in the center of the pentagram and peered inside.

Though dimmed, the picture of the forest was still visible. But this time, there was no riverbank before her. This time the waters depicted an old, thick forest with tree trunks several feet wide and thick, green moss crawling up their sides. Hard ground, years of rainfall, and brutal winds had exposed many of the tree roots, creating a thick, loosely woven foundation of ivory tresses that were interspersed with a carpet of fallen leaves and verdant green moss. Lady Meaghan sat against one of the giant oaks, her body nestled into a curve in the trunk, fitted like a hand in a glove.

"Well, isn't that cozy," Morganna snarled.

She watched Meaghan stretch and then slide down towards the base of the tree, resting her head against a mound of soft moss.

"Are we lying down for a good night's sleep?" Morganna asked. "Are we hoping for pleasant dreams?"

She smiled wickedly. "Well, then, why don't I just tuck you in nice and tight?"

Chapter Twenty-nine

Meaghan stretched and yawned. The day had been exhausting, and they had all agreed to be ready to go at first light. So, she really needed to get some sleep.

The Eochaidh were resting on the other side of the copse of trees, giving her a little privacy but positioning themselves close enough to protect her.

She slid down towards the base of the tree and laid her head on a small knob of moss and dirt. It was surprisingly comfortable. Then she wrapped her arms around herself to try and ward off some of the night's chill.

"Are you warm enough?" Tristan asked, coming from around the tree.

She looked up at the man, trying to determine if she could discern the newest signs of aging.

"You really need to stop changing," she chided mildly.

He came forward and unhooked his thick cape, then gently laid it over her. "If I didn't change, I couldn't offer you this," he replied with a smile.

Meaghan snuggled under the cloak's weight and warmth. She inhaled Tristan's unique scent, and her heart fluttered once again. "Thank you," she replied. "I'm much warmer already."

"Sweet dreams, Lady Meaghan," Tristan said, turning back to join the others.

"Sweet dreams, Sir Tristan," she replied.

Her eyes were already growing heavy. The weight of the cape and the masculine scent that encircled her gave her a feeling of security that she hadn't felt in days. Was it wrong to dream of him, she wondered. She inhaled his scent once more and wondered if she really had any choice in the matter.

With a smile on her face, she yawned, closed her eyes and drifted to sleep, dreaming of knights in shining armor.

A few feet away from where she slept, the thick, brown carpet of leaves began to softly rustle. Then, a few feet in another direction, the leaves also moved. Soon, the entire tree was surrounded by little pockets of quiet movement.

Then the fixed rustling changed as subtle movements underneath the carpet began to appear and rise up. Small tunnels, like snakes, slithered toward the tree. They slid forward, quiet and hidden as they moved closer. Finally, like a gnarled, white finger, one appeared from beneath the leaves. It slid over the stone that blocked its path and slipped down the other side, several other thick, white shoots sprouting from its main root.

The roots wove up and across each other, covering the ground and the roots of the tree where Meaghan rested in the thick, white cape. Then the first one reached the hem of the cape. It paused and lifted toward the sky, in a nearly human movement. Then it dove down and slipped underneath the cover of the cape.

Soon, gnarled, white roots came from every direction, slipped under the cape, and made their way toward the sleeping woman.

Meaghan knew she was dreaming.

She was walking through a meadow, hand in hand with Tristan. The grass was so thick and tall she could feel it wind its way around her feet and her legs. But it didn't matter. He was there with her. He turned her in his arms and looked deeply into her eyes. His hand snaked around her arm, then her waist and finally tightened, pulling her against him.

She tried to speak, but his hold was too tight. She couldn't breathe. Her joy turned to horror as she felt him squeezing the life from her.

She woke, her eyes wide with shock as she realized she couldn't move her arms, couldn't move her head. She tried to struggle, but she was caught tight.

Finally, she opened her mouth as she felt her throat closing and screamed, but the sound was a breathless moan in the wind. Her eyes dimmed. Her breath grew shallow, and she could struggle no more.

Chapter Thirty

Tristan woke, his heart pounding in terror. "Meaghan," he cried, standing and changing from horse to man as he ran through the woods, the light of the moon guiding his way.

"What is it, man?" Rufus called after him, struggling to stand and then running after him.

The rest of the knights woke and followed Tristan into the woods.

Tristan hurried to her side. She lay before him, motionless. He shook his head. She was finally sleeping. What was wrong with him?

"I'm sorry," he whispered to the others. "I had a dream... I thought..."

Then he moved to the side, and the moonlight illuminated her face.

"Her face is blue," Rufus exclaimed. "She's not breathing."

Tristan yanked the cape to the side and gasped when he saw that her entire body was encased in roots, a cocoon of thick, white strands. He and Rufus dove to the ground, grabbing the roots that encircled her neck and ripped them away.

Kneeling beside her, he watched for signs of life. She was still motionless—too still to be alive. Tristan's heart dropped.

"We're too…" he began.

Suddenly, Meaghan gasped for air. Gradually some of the color returned to her face.

"Thank the Lord," Rufus said, bending forward and pulling the roots away from her.

The other knights joined in, ripping and yanking at the thick ropes of root until they had released her head, shoulders and upper body. Tristan slid behind her, wrapped his arms around her waist and pulled her out of the deadly shroud.

Coughing, still gasping for air, she leaned against him for strength. "What…what happened?"

"Morganna," Garrett said angrily. "We were fools to believe that she wouldn't discover that you were still alive."

She lifted her hand to her throat, felt the raw welts and shuddered. "Well, we know now," she whispered, trying to be brave as her heart pounded in reaction.

"This is too dangerous," Tristan said. "We can't allow you to continue on this quest."

Still recovering, she pushed against him weakly and shook her head. "You can't allow me?" she whispered hoarsely. "I do not recall asking your permission to come."

He leaned forward so they were nearly forehead to forehead. "You are under my protection," he insisted.

"Wonderful job thus far," she retorted and felt immediate remorse when she saw his face whiten.

She placed her hand on his chest. "I apologize," she murmured. "That was not only unkind it was also untrue. You saved my life, and I just acted as an ungrateful wretch."

He stepped away from her slowly, easing her against the tree for support, and shook his head. "No, you have the right of it," he said. "I have witnessed the machinations of Morganna for over a thousand years. I should not have allowed my guard to be down. I should have known…"

"Are you a prophet now?" Rufus asked. "One who can read the future or, perhaps, read minds? The lass is right. You had no part in this, except for the saving of her life."

"I still don't understand how you knew," Andrew remarked. "Another few moments and she would have—"

He stopped abruptly when Garrett slapped him on the back of his head.

"Begging your pardon, Lady Meaghan," he immediately apologized.

"I was that close to death?" Meaghan asked. "Minutes?"

Tristan sighed and nodded. "And now you see why—"

"Why I have to continue," she interrupted. "Do you really believe that if I go home like a good little girl, Morganna will not still wish for my demise?"

Duncan shrugged and nodded. "She has a valid point."

"I am the only remaining Herdin, and if I were not a threat to the spell, Morganna would not be trying so hard to kill me," she reasoned. "I have to help you break the spell, or she will hunt me until she succeeds."

Chapter Thirty-one

The dawn was barely breaking, and a symphony of birdsongs was already echoing from the tree canopy above the small company. The five large horses and Meaghan astride her own horse stood together in a small circle, debating their next steps.

"I will not be responsible for making you miss the deadline," Meaghan argued. "Sir Duncan was correct when he said getting the amulet would delay you."

Duncan shook his head, his forelock slipping over his eyes as his hair did when he was in human form. "It is true I said that," he reasoned. "But theoretically, if we make it to the castle ruins on time and you are not there, our journey will have been for naught."

"We could split up," Rufus said. "Some with Lady Meaghan and some toward the castle."

Meaghan shook her head. "No, it will still attract undue attention," she argued. "A rider with several large horses. I really need to go alone."

"I don't like it," Garrett said. "You're already a target. There's no need for you to make yourself easy prey for Morganna."

"I think Lady Meaghan is right," Tristan said.

There was shocked silence from the other Eochaidh. And Meaghan had to admit that, although she had argued to go on her own, she'd done so out of duty, not bravery.

But, she nodded her head. "See, Sir Tristan agrees," she said. "So, I'll just be…"

Tristan moved to the side, blocking Meaghan from retreating. "You didn't let me finish," he said. "She's right that a group of large horses, even two or three, traveling with a lone rider will look suspicious. We might as well all go with her if we were to send any."

Duncan shook his head. "Excellent point," he said.

"She needs to be a lone rider, riding one horse," Tristan said.

"So you said," Meaghan said, feeling a little put-out that he was ready to send her out on her own so easily. "If you'll just move over, I'll be on my way."

"But the horse will not be your mare," Tristan continued as if he hadn't heard her.

"What?" she exclaimed.

"You'll be riding me," he said. "And your horse can go with the rest of the company."

She shook her head. "Oh, I don't like that idea at all," she said, afraid that her feelings for Tristan might be betrayed.

"It makes perfect sense," Duncan said. "You'll have protection, and we can move quickly to the ruins."

Meaghan searched her brain for a logical reason it would not work and finally came up with one. She smiled with relief. "Well, that would have been a good idea," she said. "But, a woman riding a horse as big as you, well, that would draw undue attention. It would be almost as bad as all of us going together. I really should just ride my own horse."

"Actually, I thought of that," Tristan said.

Of course you did, Meaghan thought.

"I believe we need a disguise for Lady Meaghan," Tristan announced. "Something that will cover her…" He paused, not knowing how to politely phrase his request.

"Hair?" Rufus asked with a bit of a tease in his voice. "Aye, she needs to look more like a lad than a lady." He turned to Meaghan. "Have you the clothes you used to wear when you were meeting your father in the forest?"

She shook her head. "No, I've only my sword and my tunic with the Herdin coat-of arms."

"Well, I suppose it's time to do some shopping," Garrett said. He looked around the group, and his eyes fell upon Duncan. "And you, Master Scholar, are the best one for the task."

"Me?" Duncan stammered. "I know nothing about shopping for women's things."

"It wouldn't be women's things," Garrett corrected him. "It would be a lad's clothing, and you would be the best to look over at a clothes line to determine which garments would best hide Lady Meaghan's…charms."

Meaghan blushed. "Really, no, this is…"

"Important," Tristan interrupted. "Morganna will not think twice about a country lad riding a plow horse down the road. It's the best plan we have."

Duncan turned from a horse to a man and shrugged his shoulders as he walked over to help Meaghan down from her horse. "Shall we go shopping, milady," he asked with a slight bow.

She couldn't help but smile. "Aye, it would be my pleasure, good sir," she replied.

Chapter Thirty-two

The formerly pristine stable of the Herdin estate was now a staging area for the items that had been recovered from the fire. Stacks of wooden crates filled with glassware, items from the kitchen, and paintings that had not been destroyed were in one corner. Piles of furniture that were unsinged and only held the smell of smoke stood in other areas. But, Jepson noticed, the stalls that had held the Herdin family horses were neat and clean, and the horses were well-groomed and cared for. Jepson, Fitz, and Monty were gathered in the stable.

A few of the grooms that had worked under Jepson ran towards him in greeting.

"Go," Fitz encouraged. "Speak to them and watch the grounds to make sure that young Monty and I are undisturbed."

Understanding, Jepson nodded and led the grooms outside in front of the stable, leaving the two other men alone.

"You asked me what I know of Morganna," Monty said, shaking his head in confusion. "I must say that I find that an odd question from the Herdin butler."

"Things aren't always as they seem," Fitz replied. "But you haven't answered my question."

Monty shrugged. "She's the evil witch in the fairy tale of the Eochaidh," he said. "She betrayed King Arthur. She became powerful enough to frighten Merlin."

"She never frightened Merlin," Fitz corrected immediately.

"Okay, she became powerful, and she wanted more power," he said casually. "She found a spell that would allow her to travel into the future. Some knights found out about it. She cursed them to die, but Merlin saved them by turning them into horses. Does that about do it?"

Fitz shook his head. "Not quite," he said slowly. "She came forward in time because she was able to discern when the spell had the best chance of being broken. She knew the family that could destroy her, the Herdin family. But she needed a plan. So, she met a naïve Lord who was taken by her beauty. She manipulated him and flattered him, so much so that he betrayed his own betrothed and married her."

"How odd," Monty said easily. "My own father betrayed his fiancée in order to marry…"

The words died in his throat, and he met Fitz's eyes.

Fitz nodded slowly.

"No," Monty said, but the truth rang in his heart. He walked away from Fitz, his boots clattering on the wooden floor of the stable. Then he quickly turned and walked back.

"It's a child's tale," he exclaimed. "That's all it is, a child's tale. There is no truth to it."

Fitz stepped away from Monty and walked to the pile of boxes in the corner. He pulled out a painting that had been darkened with soot and, with his hand, carefully exposed the painting underneath.

"Do you know what this is?" he asked Monty, carrying the painting over to him.

"Yes, I rescued it myself," Monty replied. "It's the painting that was over the mantle in Lord John's study. It's the Herdin coat-of-arms."

"And what does it say?" Fitz asked.

Monty brushed away the remaining bits of soot so he could read the writing more clearly. "Pura Cordis," he read slowly. Then he looked up at Fitz with disbelief in his eyes. "Pure heart."

"Do you still believe this is nothing but a child's tale?" Fitz asked.

"My mother?" Monty stammered, his voice hoarse and his eyes wide with horror. "My mother killed the Herdins? Lord John? Lady Evaleen? Meaghan?" he shook his head in denial, but Fitz could see the reflection of horror in his eyes when he accepted the truth.

Bending at the waist, physically ill, he gasped. "I can't... I can't..."

He shook his head and looked up at Fitz, his eyes brimming with tears. He had no words. The emotional hit that felt like someone had punched him in the stomach was the truth. Fitz was telling the truth. His mother was a murderer, a monster. And he was the son of a monster.

With heart-breaking sorrow, he turned and walked away from Fitz.

Fitz watched the young man stumble away, his head bowed, and his arms wrapped around his waist. Monty stopped at Galahad's stall and leaned against the thick beams that encircled the opening. The giant stallion came forward and nuzzled Monty's head, nickering softly, somehow understanding his pain. Unconsciously, the young man reached up and stroked the stallion's forelock as he stared, sightlessly, across the paddocks.

Quietly, Fitz walked across the stable until he was standing behind Monty. He studied the young man for a long moment and finally asked, "Do you believe me?"

Monty inhaled sharply and nodded sadly. "How can I not?" he replied in a whisper. "More and more, I have found myself surprised, no, dismayed by my mother's actions. By her lack of compassion. By her desire for power."

He wiped his arm across his face, dashing away the tears, and turned to Fitz. "More and more I wondered how she could be my mother," he said, pain in each word. "And now I wonder what kind of evil dwells in my own heart."

Fitz reached over and placed his arm on Monty's shoulder. "The fact that you would ask yourself that question," Fitz said kindly, "tells me more about your character than anything else you could do."

Monty shook his head. "I don't understand," he said.

"Lady Meaghan is alive," Fitz replied. "She was not home when the explosion occurred."

"No," Monty replied. "I found her." His voice broke, and he had to wait a moment before he could speak. "I carried her outside in my arms. She was wearing…"

"The rose silk dress," Fitz said softly, nodding his head. "She had given the dress to Daisy that afternoon."

"Daisy?" Monty replied incredulously. "Daisy is buried…"

"In Lady Meaghan's grave," Fitz said. "And Lady Meaghan is traveling to find the Eochaidh in order to stop Morganna."

Instantly, the young man straightened. The sorrow and regret were gone from his face. Instead, his eyes were now clear and determined. "What can I do to help?"

Chapter Thirty-three

Meaghan and Duncan scrambled across the rutted, plowed field and ducked behind the hedgerows at the edge of the farmer's yard. Though it was still early, the rooster's incessant crowing a testimony to this fact, there were an assortment of garments hanging on the clothes line.

"They look to be the right size, milady," Duncan said, squinting his eyes and peering through the bushes.

"Sir Duncan," Meaghan replied, concern in her voice. "You are looking at the bedsheets." She decided to voice the concern she'd had ever since they left the camp. "Are you, perhaps, having trouble with your vision?"

Duncan sighed and nodded. "Aye, milady," he confessed. "My glasses do not seem as powerful as they once were. I have hypothesized that it could be the age of the glass and the atmospheric conditions that have caused this."

Meaghan nodded and hid her smile. "Or it could be that you are aging, and your eyesight is getting worse," she suggested.

He turned to her, surprise on his face. "I cannot believe that I did not come to that conclusion myself," he said, a wry smile on his face. "That makes perfect sense."

"Which means we need to hurry about our task and get you back with the rest of the Eochaidh," she replied.

They watched the farmer's wife exit the back of the cottage and hurry towards the chicken house, a large pan of scraps in her hands.

"She's feeding the chickens," Meaghan said. "Now is our time to move."

Duncan hesitated. "Lady Meaghan," he confessed, looking embarrassed, "never in my life have I stolen anything. I truly wonder if this is the right thing to do."

Meaghan glanced over at the woman still walking to the chicken coop. They still had a few minutes, but not much more time than that.

"Sir Duncan, if we ask these good people for some clothing and Morganna discovers that they've helped us, they could be killed for their kindness," she explained.

She stood up, and he followed her.

"So, in a way, stealing is the honorable thing to do?" he suggested hopefully as they pushed their way through the tall bushes.

She smiled. "Aye, it is," she agreed. "And even more honorable because it goes so much against your natural tendencies."

His smile widened. "So, I'm a hero," he replied. "One could say that I was a hero."

"Yes," she said, turning so he couldn't see her smile. "One could, indeed, say that."

They reached the edge of the bushes and peered around. The woman was still in with the chickens.

"Let's go," Meaghan whispered urgently.

They dashed across the yard to the cover of the bed sheets flapping in the wind. Pressed against the woven material, they slowly made their way down the line to the clothing. There were several shirts and pants that would have fit Meaghan and one of the Eochaidh at the same time. *The farmer is certainly a burly man*, Meaghan thought.

Then a little farther down the line was a shirt and breeches that looked just about her size. She grabbed them, and Duncan tried to follow her but got tangled up in one of the sheets. Meaghan turned to help him and closed her eyes in dismay when she heard the cry of the farmer's wife.

"Hey! Hold on there!" the woman cried. "Take your hands off my laundry."

Meaghan turned to meet the woman who, upon closer inspection, seemed a good match for her husband. She hoped that she wasn't going to get her ears boxed by this good homemaker.

"You no good gypsies," the woman shouted, observing Meaghan's dress and shawl.

Not wanting the gypsies to be blamed, Meaghan dropped the shawl and exposed her fair skin and auburn locks. "No, good lady, not a gypsy," she replied. "Just a poor miss on the run."

"On the run?" the woman asked, eyeing Meaghan carefully. "From who?"

Just then Duncan found his way out of the sheet and landed in a pile at Meaghan's feet. "I'm out!" he exclaimed proudly.

"And who is this charlatan?" the woman demanded.

Meaghan closed her eyes for a moment, sending up a quick prayer for forgiveness for lying. Then she opened them and turned to the woman. "He's my betrothed," she said.

"I'm your what?" Duncan exclaimed, and Meaghan kicked him lightly. "It's fine, Duncan. We can tell this lovely woman the truth."

His widened eyes closed slightly, and he nodded slowly. "Of course," he said. "I just didn't want to give away our secret."

The woman looked at the young, beautiful woman and the older, scholarly looking fellow and shook her head. "You're engaged to him?" she asked, astonished.

"He was my tutor," Meaghan lied. "And, I believe, it was love at first sight. But, even though my Duncan is a good man, my father has promised me to the old Earl."

"The old Earl, you say," the woman repeated, leaning towards Meaghan. "How old would he be?"

Meaghan bowed her head and whimpered slightly. She peeked up at the woman. "He's had six so far. When he wed his last wife, it was rumored that he had reached his sixtieth year. But he keeps his age a secret. I can only guess."

"Six wives?" she replied, astonished. "Why so many?"

Meaghan shuddered delicately. "I understand that if they do not produce an heir within a certain amount of time," she whispered, "they are met with suspicious deaths."

The woman placed her hands on her ample hips. "And what kind of father would marry his daughter off to such a fiend?" she asked, angry at the unseen patriarch.

Meaghan pulled her handkerchief from her pocket and dabbed at her eyes. "One who was foolish enough to participate in a game of chance with the old Earl," she explained. "He didn't realize that the old Earl is known for his chicanery."

The old woman nodded sagely. "Cheated your old man, did he?"

"Yes," Meaghan replied. "And left me with no other choice but to escape the situation with my beloved Duncan."

The woman looked down at Duncan and shook her head. "So, he was the best ship in a storm, eh?" she muttered, and then she shook her head. "Well, then, what do you need?"

Meaghan smiled at the woman. "I thought if I could disguise myself as a lad, we might be able to travel unnoticed," she said.

"Well, nothing on the line is going to help you," she said. "That linen shirt you have is thin enough to see through. That won't do at all. Whilst your young man pulls himself up off the ground, why don't you come up to the house with me. I'm sure we got something that will suit you just fine."

Chapter Thirty-four

Several minutes later, Meaghan emerged from the farmhouse dressed in dark brown breeches, a thick, homespun shirt, a thick, wool vest, a pair of knee-high leather boots and a large felt hat that was large enough to hide all her hair while the wide-brim hid most of her face.

Duncan met her at the base of the small stoop on the outside of the house and studied her slowly. Then he took off his glasses, rubbed them on his shirt and placed them on his nose once again. He shook his head. "No, there's something still a little off here," he said. "The clothing certainly has the look of a lad. But the clothing on you does not say lad at all. Begging your pardon, mi…" He paused and corrected himself. "Meaghan."

Meaghan turned back to the farmer's wife. "What do you think?" she asked.

The woman stepped forward and untucked the shirt from the waistband of the breeches, leaving it loose and flowing. "There you are," she said. "Keep that shirt loose so your figure don't show so much."

Meaghan smiled and nodded. "Thank you," she said, and then she turned to Duncan. "Better?"

He nodded. "Yes, much better."

Turning back to the farmer's wife, Meaghan reached and slipped a gold coin into her hand. "Thank you so much for helping me," she said.

The woman looked down at the coin, and her eyes widened with shock. "Oh, no, I can't take this from you," she protested. "It's far too much."

Meaghan shook her head. "No, it is just right," she said. "Not only for the clothing but also for the friendship and advice. Please take it."

The woman took only a moment to decide and then slid the coin into her ample bosom. "Well," she said with a satisfied smile. "If you insist."

Meaghan smiled back. "I do," she said. "Thank you for your help. And now, we must really hurry on before my father comes after me."

"Yes, you go on," the woman said. Then she glanced at Duncan and lowered her voice. "And remember what I said to you."

"I will," Meaghan said with an earnest nod to her new friend. "And thank you."

A few minutes later, when Duncan and Meaghan were walking side by side hiking down the narrow path in the woods, Duncan turned to her. "What advice did she give you?" he asked.

Meaghan smiled fondly at the memory of the woman's words. "She said that I should always choose love," she said. "Even though it might not be the easy choice."

"What a wise woman," Duncan replied. "Through all my years of study, I have discovered that wisdom is often found in the most unexpected places."

Meaghan's smile widened. "I have found more wisdom from the people who live closer to the earth than any so-called educated or sophisticated folk," she said. "I would take Mrs. Gallagher's ointments and tinctures over something a physician suggested in a heartbeat."

Then she remembered, and her heart broke all over again. Never again would Mrs. Gallagher rub her sweet-smelling ointment on Meaghan's cuts or bruises. Never again would she be fed a spoonful of elderberry syrup to ease her colds. Never again would she help her gather wild herbs in the forest. The loss suddenly seemed too deep and overwhelming.

"What is it, milady?" Duncan asked, noticing the sudden change in Meaghan's mood.

She shook her head and whisked the tears from her cheeks. "Mrs. Gallagher was in the house when it was destroyed," she whispered. "Another innocent life Morganna destroyed for power."

Duncan nodded. "I'm sorry for your loss, milady," he said gently. "I cannot imagine the pain of your heart."

Summoning a smile, she turned to him. "Thank you for your kind words," she replied mechanically.

"I know they are just words, milady," Duncan replied. "And they cannot change what has occurred. But I pray that they will be a bit of balm for your grief."

She paused for a moment and realized that his words had helped. The pain in her heart had lessened slightly. "They did help," she said to him. "Thank you for them."

Chapter Thirty-five

"Hurry. Hurry. Hurry!" Morganna exclaimed as she looked down in the scrying bowl and watched the roots slowly creep across the ground towards Meaghan. She glanced up and out the tower window. The tide was rising, and soon the isthmus would be totally covered. In the daytime travel was risky, but now, at night, driving through the water would be suicide.

She looked back down at the bowl. The roots had begun to creep underneath Meaghan's cape, and she watched as the first one stole up from beneath Meaghan's hair and crawled over her neck. She smiled and stepped away from the bowl, satisfied that her spell would take care of the young woman.

"And now, there are a few other loose ends I must attend to," she said, walking to the curving stairs and hurrying down.

"Bring the carriage," she yelled. "We must depart immediately!"

A few minutes later, after the carriage had driven through the foaming seawater, it stopped on the edge of the road near the young yew tree. Morganna, dressed as Lady Strathmore, stepped down from the carriage and turned to her henchmen. "Get rid of that corpse in my potion chamber," she ordered. "I won't have need of it any longer." She smiled wickedly. "After I deal with my son, I won't have to go back to that time and place ever again."

"Yes, Lady Morganna," he replied. "I'll take care of it immediately."

She nodded, pleased. "See that you do," she said. "I don't like being disappointed."

He shuddered automatically and then bowed to try and disguise it. "Yes, milady," he said. "You won't be disappointed."

She walked away from him without another word and knelt by the yew. Moments after she whispered the words to the spell, she was gone.

The henchman breathed a sigh of relief.

"What's that she said about her son?" the driver of the carriage asked, leaning over the side.

The henchman shook his head. "She said she needed to deal with him," he repeated. "That don't bode well for him."

The driver shook his head. "Naw, he's her own flesh and blood," he disagreed. "She ain't likely to kill her own flesh and blood."

The henchman turned and looked up at the driver. "You ain't been here too long, have you?" he asked, shaking his head and climbing onto the back of the carriage.

Chapter Thirty-six

The road was uneven, rocky and dry. A cloud of dust surrounded them as Tristan cantered down the middle of it. Meaghan sneezed. She let go of Tristan's mane with one hand and tried to wave the dust away from her face. She was riding bareback because her horse's saddle had not been large enough to fit on Tristan. Likewise, the reins were too small, so she held tightly to his mane.

"Can't we just slow down long enough for me to breathe a little fresh air?" she asked the horse.

He slowed his pace. The dust slowly cleared, and she could finally see the blue sky.

"The dust wasn't bothering me," he said.

She rolled her eyes. "That's because your nose and eyes are in front of your hooves," she said, "so the dust is formed behind you, where I'm sitting."

"I've never had any complaints before," he replied.

"And how many people have actually ridden you before me?" she asked.

He was silent for a moment, and all that was heard was the clopping of his hooves against the soft dirt. Finally, he sighed. "You have the right of it," he said. "My primary concern is to reach the others as soon as possible."

Meaghan nodded, even though she knew he couldn't see it. She found it much easier to converse with Tristan as a horse than as a man. When he was a man, she found his presence to be quite unnerving.

"Do you find it odd to be speaking with a horse?" he asked.

She smiled, wondering if he could read her thoughts. "No, actually, I've always spoken to my horse," she replied, and then she shrugged. "The only odd thing in this current situation is that the horse is responding back to me."

He chuckled softly, and Meaghan was surprised it didn't come out as a nicker. "You don't, er…" she said and then paused, trying to come up with the correct phrasing. "You don't speak horse?"

He laughed. This time it was deep and masculine, and it sent a delighted shiver through Meaghan's body. "No, milady, I have never learned horse," he replied. "Because we travel together and remain hidden as much as possible, we rarely have to rely on that kind of subterfuge."

"But if…" she paused when she heard the sound of hoofbeats approaching. "Someone's coming."

He shook his head, his mane flouncing in the air, and continued forward, his head held high and his ears turned forward and alert.

Meaghan pulled her hat tighter over her hair and checked to be sure her shirt and vest still concealed the fact that she was a woman. Then she sat tall in the saddle and looked over Tristan's head. Coming up the road towards them were three large men on sway-backed, worn and dirty horses.

"Well, they can't outrun us," she whispered, and Tristan nodded his head.

As they came closer, one of the men dismounted and walked toward her. Meaghen grabbed tight to Tristan's mane as he moved slightly to the side of the road.

"Nice horse," the man said.

Meaghan nodded but said nothing.

"Cat got your tongue, boy?" the man asked.

"Not supposed to talk to strangers," Meaghan said, keeping her voice low.

"Oh, we ain't strangers," the man replied. "We're the folks who want to buy your horse from you."

"He ain't for sale," Meaghan said.

Tristan pawed the air and blew angrily through his nostrils.

"He sure got spirit," the man replied. "Too much spirit for a lad like you."

Meaghan saw that the two other men were moving their horses on either side of the road, as if they were trying to surround them.

The man on the road stepped forward, and Tristan moved back. "Hey there," the man said calmly to Tristan. "Don't you worry. I'm your friend."

"We don't need friends," Meaghan replied, turning slightly to face the man.

At that moment, Tristan lunged forward to get away. Taken by surprise, Meaghan slipped off his back and landed on the road.

The man laughed at her. "You can handle him, eh?" he asked. Then, he turned to see the huge horse charging him. The man screamed and ran off the road, with Tristan running after him.

"Go, Tristan," Meaghan yelled, slowly getting to her feet and rubbing her sore behind. Then she turned to see the other two men pulling ropes from their saddles and positioning their horses closer to the man on the ground.

The man turned and ran back towards his friends with Tristan charging close behind. The other two men had their ropes looped and waiting.

"No, Tristan, no!" Meaghan screamed, running toward the men.

Tristan started to turn, but both the men threw their ropes over his head. The ropes sailed over and landed on his neck. Then both men tightened the ropes and pulled him to a skittering stop. Tristan tried to rear up, but the men had anchored the ropes to their saddles, so he couldn't raise up.

They shortened the lead until he was caught between the two horses, and they forced him to move down the road.

"Wait!" Meaghan screamed, running down the road towards him. "He's my horse. Give him back to me."

"I guess he's our horse now," the first man said, mounting his own horse. "I told you that you couldn't handle him."

Then they turned and galloped back the way they'd come.

Chapter Thirty-seven

Meaghan kept running towards them, but with Tristan caught firmly between them, they were soon out of sight. She went back and picked up the saddlebags that had been thrown with her, slipped them over her shoulder and started to walk to the nearest town.

A mile ahead, the road inclined, and when Meaghan reached the top, she could see a village in the distance. The road in front of her traveled into some woods, then skirted the boundaries of the village and finally turned into the village from the north. She was closer to the southern entrance, but there was no road. She would have to walk through several fields to get there.

Just then, she saw the three men and Tristan come out from the woods and continue north on the road. Tristan was fighting them, pulling against the ropes and slowing them down. If they were headed to the village, and Meaghan was fairly sure they were, if she cut through the fields, she could get to town at about the same time they arrived.

She dashed down the side of the road, climbed over the rock fence that enclosed the first hayfield and prayed that this field wasn't also shared with the farmer's prize bull. Just to be safe, she walked alongside the fence in case she had to make a quick escape.

The hay was high in the fields, past her waist, and smelled of sweet alfalfa. The narrow strip between the hay and the fence gave her an easy path, but it also nearly hid her from curious eyes. She jogged down the path towards a small brook and paused for a moment to get a drink. Kneeling down on the bank of the brook, she leaned forward and scooped up cold, fresh water with her hand. It felt so good trickling down her dry throat. She could feel the water slowly refreshing her body.

"You're going to need a plan."

She jumped back and looked around, her hand going to the saddlebag that held her knife. Then she paused when she saw the little man standing on the other side of the brook. He was no more than three feet tall, with white hair and a white beard that reached to his waist. His face was lined and dark brown, like an ancient oak, but his eyes were bright blue. He wore a green jacket, brown leggings and green slippers.

"Who are you?" she whispered.

"A friend," he replied with an easy smile. "Not all fae live in the forest, milady."

She sighed. "They've taken Tristan," she said.

He nodded. "Aye, I saw," he said with a twinkle in his eye. "But you fought valiantly."

She rolled her eyes. "I fell off," she said.

He laughed, and it sounded like shallow water babbling over stones, pure and clear. "You did, yes," he finally said. "But it was a valiant fall."

"I need to get him back," she said. "And I must do it quickly. We don't have a lot of time to spare."

He nodded, the laughter gone from his face. "Aye, the signs foretell the time will soon be upon us," he agreed. "And so, you must get the Eochaidh and be on your way quickly."

"Do you know those who took him?" she asked. "I would gladly purchase him from them."

"And have them steal him again once you are on the road?" he asked, shaking his head. "No, all they understand are violence and death."

"I will have to kill them?" she asked.

He shook his head. "No, milady," he replied. "But you will have to make them think that someone will. And your current disguise will not aid you in this quest. Come with me. I have a fondness for lovely things, and I'm sure there will be something in my collection that will help you."

She waded across the river and followed him to a small copse of trees at the edge of one of the fields. In the center was a large, ancient oak whose limbs spread out for several yards in all directions and were so heavy they nearly touched the ground. He walked to the trunk and placed his hand on the ragged back. The tree shook slightly, and then a small doorway was revealed. He pulled open the door and turned to her. "This way, milady."

She stooped over and followed him inside, expecting a tiny chamber. Instead, she walked into a huge chamber filled with untold treasure. She stood with him at the top of a marble staircase that looked down to a room larger than her entire home. Flaming sconces on the wall illuminated the room. Open chests of jewels, gold, and silver overflowed onto the floor. There were hills of coins surrounding statues from ancient times. There were thrones and paintings, crowns and swords, every treasure she had ever imagined lay before her. She slowly took it all in and then turned to him.

"How…" she began.

He smiled at her and shook his head. "Magic often has no explanation," he said. "Now, come with me. I have the perfect disguise for you."

They walked down the curving, marble staircase, and he led her to a large armoire that was inset with gold and jewels. "This belonged to a very famous queen," he said. "She was good to the fae and understood us. Her husband, however, decided that because she could not bear him a son, he would forfeit her life."

"How awful," Meaghan exclaimed.

The little man nodded. "We brought her to the land of fae before he could kill her," he said. "And we brought her treasures too. Her disappearance, and the loss of his treasures, drove the husband slowly mad. It was enjoyable to watch."

Meaghan stopped and stared at him. She realized that the eyes she thought were kind were actually dark and cold. She shivered and wrapped her arms around herself.

He watched her, and once again, he laughed. "Oh, my dear," he said. "Do not think of me as a kindly, harmless soul. I am bloodthirsty, selfish, and sometimes cruel. But I am fair. You have always treated the fae with respect, and so, in return I will help you on your quest. But only because it suits me too."

He smiled at her.

"The fae are not sweet wee folk with pure hearts," he explained. "We are self-serving and mischievous. Do not be fooled."

She slowly shook her head. "I will try not to be," she said.

"Good," he replied, opening the armoire. "And now, here is the disguise I was looking for."

Chapter Thirty-eight

Monty lifted the collar of the coat he was wearing and brought it to his nose. "That smell! That smell that I was wondering about," he exclaimed as he rode down the lane with Jepson and Fitz. "That smell is me!"

Jepson chuckled. "Well, Boris, whose coat that used to be, had a habit of taking a nap in the stables where his wife wouldn't find him," he explained.

"I smell of a barn?" Monty cried. "No! This just won't do!" He appealed to Fitz, who was also dressed as a gypsy and was riding beside him. "I don't understand why we need these disguises. No one is after me."

Fitz continued guiding his horse down the narrow lane alongside the other two riders without answering for a few moments. Then he turned in his saddle and met Monty's eyes. "What do you know about magic?" he asked.

Monty shrugged. "It's an ability to create spells and change things at a whim," he said.

Fitz shook his head. "No, that is the practice of magic," he said. "What is magic itself?"

"I suppose it's a power. A force," Monty replied.

Fitz nodded. "Yes, that's a good description," he said. "Now let me ask you another question. Which has a greater force—gallons of water falling on a field as rain or rushing down a river?"

"The river has more power," Monty said.

"Why?"

"Because the water is contained, directed," Monty replied. "The rain drops fall on the whole field, but the river is kept within certain boundaries."

"Very good," Fitz replied. "And magic is very much like that. When it is condensed or, let's say, focused, it has a greater power than when it is just randomly released."

"That's all well and good," Monty said. "But what does that have to do with me riding about smelling of goat?"

Fitz smiled. "Bear with me for just a few more moments," he said. "When you are on a hunt with your dogs, what is one of the first things you do?"

"I let the dogs smell the scent of the game we're hunting," Monty replied.

"Why?" Fitz asked.

Monty shrugged. "I suppose it's like the magic thing again," he said. "It focuses them on one scent, one target."

"Ah, very, very well done," Fitz replied. "And magic can also have a focus or, as you so aptly described, a target. And the strongest way to focus magic is through blood."

"Blood?" Monty asked. "Why is that?"

"Because it is somewhat unique to the bearer," he replied. "A drop of your blood in a potion will most likely focus the magic directly on you."

"Most likely?" Monty asked. Then he stopped his horse in the middle of the lane and stared at Fitz. "Or it will focus on my parents because I carry their blood in my veins. I carry Morganna's blood in my veins."

"Just so," Fitz said. "And if Morganna were to tie up all of her loose ends…"

"She would want me dead," he said slowly. "My own mother would want me dead."

"This is no reflection on you," Fitz said gently. "You have already shown more compassion and empathy in your few years than she has shown over more than a thousand."

Monty focused on the road in front of him for a few minutes. Not only was Morganna his mother but she was probably trying to kill him, just as she'd killed the Herdins. He thought back to his interaction with her during the past several years. Fitz was right. She showed no compassion or empathy. She demonstrated no noblesse oblige. She merely wanted what she wanted. She was selfish, petulant and evil.

He took a deep breath. Well, he was going to do everything in his power to make sure she did not succeed. If nothing else, he owed it to his father and the Strathmore name.

Suddenly, a thought occurred to him, and he turned to Fitz.

"My father?" he asked.

"Died in a tragic accident," Fitz said. "And no one was present but your mother."

"So, she killed him too," he replied.

Fitz nodded. "There are no redeeming qualities in her soul."

"If she can play with time, then why doesn't she just go back and kill me as a child?" Monty asked.

"Because every change in a timeline changes all the events after it," Fitz said. "If she were to go back and kill you, then there is a possibility that the Herdins would not be home the night of the explosion. So, she can only alter things after the event."

"This is all very confusing," Monty said. "But I will do whatever it takes to help Meggie."

"You are indeed a good friend," Fitz said. "And that's probably exactly what she needs at this time."

Chapter Thirty-nine

"What I really need is a shawl," Meaghan muttered as she tugged on the neckline of the gown she was wearing. "How could anyone wear this and not blush?"

The gown the little man had given her was luxurious beyond her wildest dreams. With a sky blue silk underdress overlaid with pearl beading and jeweled accents, it indeed was a dress made for a queen. But it was also very low-cut in the bodice and certainly displayed more of her charms than she had ever displayed before.

She stood at the edge of the village and took a deep breath. It would never do to have the villagers see her tugging at her gown like a school-girl miss. They would never believe the plan she and the little man had concocted. She needed to act queenly. She needed, she thought with a painful twinge in her heart, to act like her mother.

She brushed away the lone tear, lifted her head and strolled into the town, heading toward the village square. The narrow road that led past the small cottages with their tiny garden plots and flower boxes reminded her of home. Behind the windows adorned with brightly colored shutters were the sounds of family—babies crying, children playing and adults laughing. Sounds that she already missed and knew she would never hear again. She suddenly understood how someone could feel isolated in the midst of hundreds of people.

As she got closer to the village square, there were more people on the road. She could hear the whispers and could feel the stares, but she could not let them distract her from her mission.

"Excuse me, your ladyship," a young woman said, bowing deeply at her feet. "May I be of service?"

Meaghan nearly laughed at the absurdity of the situation, but with a calm and polite air her mother would never have recognized from her daughter, she nodded. "Thank you, child. I seek a horse," she replied. "I was told there were traders in the area."

"Yes, your ladyship," the girl replied, remaining in her curtsy. "They are across from the blacksmith's shop in the square."

"Thank you for your help," Meaghan replied graciously.

The girl blushed and bowed lower.

Meaghan hurried away, hoping the girl didn't hurt herself by bowing for so long. "I would have already been flat on the floor," she muttered to herself as she hurried toward the square.

Sure enough, as the girl had mentioned, a makeshift paddock had been created with rope tied around four large trees. Tristan was inside of it tied to one of the trees.

Meaghan took a deep breath and walked across the street toward the three thieves who had stolen her horse. She smiled at them as she approached, and their eyes nearly popped out of their heads.

Meaghan looked past them to Tristan, willing him to look up at her. Finally, the horse lifted his head and saw her. His eyes widened, and he stared at her for a long moment. She nodded discreetly and then turned back to the three.

"Good day, gentlemen," she said, offering them her hand.

The first one grabbed it and placed a wet kiss on her knuckles. "Your ladyship," he gushed. "I've never seen such a vision in my whole life."

She hid the jolt of revulsion she felt when he touched her. Instead she smiled serenely. "Why thank you, my good sir," she replied, moving past them and situating herself so she was up against the rope fence. "I must admit that you three are my last hope." She lowered her voice and spoke confidentially.

They moved in closer, and she had to draw out her handkerchief to cover her nose and block their smell. "Please gentleman," she pleaded. "Not quite so close."

They immediately stepped back, and she sighed with relief.

"As I was saying," she continued, "you are my last hope, and I pray I can put my faith in you.

For not only do I need to purchase a horse from you I need you to be gallant and offer your lives up too."

"What?" the first man exclaimed. "Listen, your ladyship, we're fine with selling you a horse, but we ain't too keen on losing our lives. What kind of business is this?"

Meaghan stood on her toes and glanced out over their heads into the crowd. "Well, we're still quite safe," she said. Then she lowered her voice. "You have, of course, heard of Lord Tristan?"

"No, can't say we have," the first one replied.

Meaghan placed her hands behind her back and leaned against the tree, subtly searching for the rope that bound him. "Oh, dear," she said. "Well, Lord Tristan is my betrothed."

The horse whinnied behind her, and she nearly smiled. She found the rope and started to untie the knot.

"He is incredibly jealous and nearly mad," she said. "He's already beheaded four gentlemen for just glancing in my direction."

"What?" the first man shouted.

"Is that him?" Meaghan gasped, and the three men looked around. At that moment, Meaghan pulled the end of the rope through and untied the knot. She brought her hands forward and laid one on her brow. "Oh, it was not," she sighed. "I am so thankful. I truly would not want three more deaths on my hands."

"We ain't afraid of no Lord," the second man said.

She nodded. "That is wonderful to hear," she said, and then she paused thoughtfully. "Although that is what the last one said before Tristan ran him through with his sword." Then she smiled at him. "But I'm sure that you will be a much better match."

"A match?" the second man exclaimed. "What kind of match?"

"Well, you know, a duel," she said and sighed. "Tristan does love a good duel."

"I ain't—"

At that moment, Tristan bolted away from the tree, jumped over the rope fence and galloped away down the streets of the village. Meaghan looked over her shoulder and shook her head. "Was that the horse you were going to sell me?" she asked innocently.

"Yes, it was," the first man growled, slowly moving towards her. "And I'd like to know how he got away."

Meaghan met his eyes coolly. "And so would I," she replied. "Seeing as my only escape just galloped away. Have you no other horses?"

"Meaghan! Meaghan, where are you, lass?"

Meaghan gasped and put her hands over her neck. "It's Tristan!" she exclaimed. "He's found me." She turned to the men. "Please, stand and fight for me."

The three looked at each other and then at the man walking down the middle of the street towards them. They could see that he was no local farmer or tradesman. This was a man trained in the art of warfare.

The first man looked at Meaghan and weighed his options. This woman was probably worth her weight in gold if her gown was any measure of her coffers. And she would be grateful for their help. He licked his lips and nodded. Probably very grateful.

"Ho, lads," he said to his companions. "There's three of us and only one of him. We can take 'im for sure."

"You sure 'bout this?" the second one asked, looking at his friend in disbelief.

"Yeah, come on, it'll be fun!" the first cried.

They all picked up long, thick staffs and walked toward Tristan. Tristan paused for a moment, looked around and saw a similar staff lying next to a farmer's booth. "May I purchase this?" he asked the farmer.

With a toothless grin, the farmer shook his head. "I've waited a long time fer those blokes to get some comeuppance," he whispered with a twinkle in his eyes. "Go ahead and take it. And beat the stuffin' out of them boys."

Smiling, he nodded at the farmer, picked up the heavy staff and walked back to the center of the road.

The men approached Tristan, each brandishing their staff in both hands. Tristan took a firm hold of his staff with both hands on one end and then planted his feet firmly onto the road.

The first man ran towards him, his staff raised over his head and his eyes narrowed and determined. As he got closer, he bent at the waist, like a bull charging at a target.

Meaghan swallowed nervously as she watched. The ruffian outweighed Tristan by at least one hundred pounds, and Tristan wasn't moving. She clasped her hands together and held her breath as she waited for impact.

But there was no impact. At the last second, Tristan stepped to the side, and the man fell forward with Tristan's staff slapping against his backside to help him on his way. He landed in the dirt and slid for several feet, his chin leading the way. He lay motionless in the dirt for a few moments. Then, finally, he pushed himself up and shook his head. He stood slowly and turned towards Tristan.

"You won't do that to me again," he growled, and with the staff raised over his head, he charged.

Tristan waited until the last moment again, but this time, he pivoted and whipped the staff against the back of the ruffian's knees. The force dropped the man immediately. Then Tristan knocked the staff from his arms and held his own staff against his face.

"Shall we continue?" he asked mildly.

The man glanced at his friends. "Come on," he cried. "Attack him!"

The other two looked at each other in horror and then turned to their friend. "We ain't gonna get beat up for no fancy lady," the second one exclaimed. "We got no problem with him."

The second man turned to Meaghan. "Sorry, your ladyship," he said. "We don't want no part of this."

The two of them turned and ran down the road in the opposite direction.

Tristan looked down at the man in front of him. "Would you like to join your friends?" he asked.

The man nodded eagerly. "Yes, milord," he pled. "It weren't my idea in the first place." He nodded in Meaghan's direction. "It were all her idea. That's the truth of it."

Tristan lowered his staff and stepped back. "Well, then," he said. "Off with you."

Lumbering up, the man quickly brushed himself off and ran down the street after his friends.

"You just can't get good help these days, can you?" Tristan asked, a smile on his face as he walked over and offered Meaghan his arm.

She shrugged and smiled back at him. "No, you can't," she chuckled back. "And it's even harder to find a good horse."

They walked together past the square and away from the crowds. Then he turned to her. "I must compliment you on your attire, milady," he said softly, admiration evident in his eyes.

She blushed and curtsied. "Why thank you, milord," she said. "It was given to me by a friend who fights the same battle we fight." She shrugged casually. "At least for the time being."

He stepped closer to her and cradled her face in his hand. "I also must tell you that my heart dropped when I saw you walking towards those men," he whispered. "Had they harmed you…"

"But, they did not," she replied. "And I had a plan."

He smiled, and she marveled at the fine lines that now extended from his eyes. "So you did," he said, moving a step closer.

She shivered. "What are you doing?" she asked.

He turned her so her back was to the village. "Since you told them I was your betrothed, I feel we must continue the charade, in case they are watching."

"Are they watching?" She tried to turn her head, but he held it steady.

"Don't look," he said. "They will be suspicious."

"Oh," she breathed softly as he lifted his other hand up to cradle her face. "What are…"

He softly pressed his lips against hers, barely touching, barely tasting.

She moaned softly, and he was lost. He pulled her against him and crushed his lips against hers. She clutched his shoulders and held on as the maelstrom of his kiss tossed her emotions like a ship in the storm.

Finally, he slowed, showering light and gentle kisses on her face. Then he looked down at her and nearly lost himself again when he saw the desire in her eyes and her lips, bee-stung with his kisses. And the innocence. He closed his eyes and berated himself for taking advantage of her innocence. He could not offer for her. He could not stay with her. If they fell in love, he could only break her heart—and his own, he admitted to himself.

"Tristan," she sighed, confused and stirred.

He took a shaky breath and stepped away. "They're gone now," he replied, praying she wouldn't hear the tremor in his voice. "We're safe."

"Safe?" she asked, confused.

He nodded. "Yes, the kiss looks like it did the trick," he replied.

"Trick?" she replied. Had this only been a trick? Had the kiss meant nothing to him? Was she just one in a long line of women? She stepped back, trying to shore up the pain she was feeling. Then she took a deep breath and nodded.

"Well, good," she said, tamping down her emotions. "Then we should be off. We've wasted enough time."

She turned from him and continued quickly up the street.

He started to call out, wanting to apologize. Even more than that, he wanted to pull her into his arms once again. But he knew that there was nothing but pain in a relationship that was doomed to end with either death or a thousand years distance.

With a bowed head, he followed her to the village's edge.

Chapter Forty

Lady Strathmore whisked into the manor house and quickly looked around. Monty was not in the front parlor where he normally sat eating a snack at this hour. She walked into the dining room. The plates from breakfast were still out, untouched. A feeling of unease settled in her stomach. She went to the bell pull and yanked, summoning her butler.

"Yes, milady," the butler intoned, slightly short of breath from running from the front of the house at her summons.

"I wish to see the new Earl," she demanded. "Bring Monty to me at once."

The butler closed his eyes in regret for a brief moment, took a deep breath and nodded. "The Earl is not at home, milady," he replied. "He is out looking over his other interests."

Her eyes wide with anger, Lady Strathmore turned to the butler. "His other interests?" she asked. "His other interests? And just what might those other interests be?"

The butler, his heart pounding in his chest, stood his ground. "I'm afraid he did not elaborate, milady," he replied.

She stared at the servant for several long moments. "Was he accompanied by anyone?" she asked, her voice seething.

The butler swallowed audibly and then nodded. "Yes, milady," he said. "He had servants from the Herdin estate with him."

"The former Herdin estate," Lady Strathmore corrected automatically. Then she paused, a terrified look in her eyes.

"Which servants?" she demanded.

"I believe it was the butler and the head groom," he replied.

Her scream of anger echoed throughout the entire house. She slapped the old butler across the face in her rage. "Get me a silver bowl and a pitcher of water," she shrieked. "And bring them to my sitting room immediately. Do you understand?"

He nodded. "Yes, milady, immediately."

She stormed up the stairs to her sitting room and threw open the double doors with enough force to make them crash against the walls and spring back together. With one swipe of her arm, she cleared the top of her vanity, sending crystal bottles and delicate, hand-blown vases to the floor in a shattered heap.

Turning, she impatiently went to the door. "What's taking so long?" she demanded. She watched with livid eyes as the butler and maid ran down the hall carrying the bowl and the water.

"Put it on my vanity and leave me," she ordered.

Only too happy to be out of her presence, the two quickly deposited their burdens on the vanity and rushed from the room. Lady Strathmore slammed the doors behind them and locked them securely. Then she took her traveling hat from her head and tossed it across the room on her way back to the vanity.

Setting the bowl in the middle of the vanity, she slowly poured the water in, murmuring the same words she'd used in her tower room. Once the water was in the bowl, she put the pitcher down, opened a small drawer in the vanity and pulled out a delicate, ivory handled knife. Holding one hand over the bowl, she ran the knife along her palm, a line of bright red blood appearing behind the tip. She squeezed her hand into a tight fist, and drops of blood splashed onto the surface of the water, slowly spreading in minute droplets over the surface.

Wrapping her hand in a handkerchief, she looked back down into the bowl. "Blood of my blood," she whispered. "Show me my son."

The water darkened for a moment, and then ripples ran from the center of the bowl to the outside rim. Finally, the water cleared, and Lady Strathmore could see Monty riding alongside Fitz and Jepson as they traveled down the country road.

"On your way to see other interests? You dare toy with me?" she spat. "I had planned to kill you in your sleep, my son. But now your death will be slow and painful."

Chapter Forty-one

Tristan and Meaghan walked along the road in silence, each lost in their own thoughts, when they came across a copse of trees. Tristan stopped and looked behind them. "This might be the best place to change," he suggested.

Meaghan nodded and took the saddlebags from Tristan. "I'll only be a moment," she said.

"I'll stay on the road and watch," he replied. "And when you're done, I'll change."

She pushed her way through the brush and found an area that was protected on all sides where she could change. She was unbuttoning her gown when she realized she was not alone.

"Well met, milady," said the little man who had helped her earlier. "I see our plan worked."

She nodded and smiled at him. "It did, yes," she said. "Thank you for your aid."

He bowed slightly. "It was my pleasure," he said.

"If you'll give me just a moment, I'll return your gown to you," she said.

He nodded and turned around to give her privacy. She slipped out of the gown and put the clothing she had purchased from the farm woman back on. "Here you are," she said, carefully offering him the gown. "Thank you again."

"That was very nicely done, milady," he said. "And now, I have a gift for you."

"But I am in your debt," she argued. "I couldn't accept another gift."

He pulled a silver sword from behind his back and held it up to her. "This is not just for you," he explained. "This is for all who refuse to bend to Morganna's will and who desire to be out from under her shadow."

Meaghan took the sword and held it up. "It is so light," she replied, amazed.

"Its material is not of your world," he said. "It was cast in the same fires as Excalibur, although it was always meant for a lady warrior." He paused and studied her for a long moment. "I believe it was always meant for you."

She grasped the hilt and suddenly felt a surge of power in her arm. Gasping softly, she stared in wonder at the sword.

"Ah, you feel the magic," he said with a satisfied nod. "Good. Good. I was not wrong in my choice of a gift."

"But how do I use it?" she asked.

He smiled at her and then stepped back, nearly disappearing into the greenery. "You will know," he said. "I wish you success in fulfilling your quest."

Then he was gone.

Meaghan shook her head in amazement, then turned to go back to the road when she noticed a woman's belt and scabbard on the ground near the saddlebags. She picked it up and smiled. "You think of everything, don't you," she murmured. "Thank you."

She put the belt around her hips and adjusted it so it fit snugly. Then she placed the small sword

235

inside the scabbard. When she pulled her shirt over them both, it nearly hid all of the sword. "Well, that works nicely."

She picked up the saddlebags and pushed her way out through the brush to the road.

"Is everything fine?" Tristan asked when she walked back to the road.

"The little man who helped me earlier appeared in the woods," she explained. "I was able to return the dress to him."

Tristan swung around and faced the woods. "You should have called out," he said. "I would have been—"

"He's a friend," Meaghan interrupted, calming him. "He is on our side in this quest. There was no need to call you."

"Meaghan, I want to protect you," he insisted.

Meaghan smiled sadly and shook her head. "We both know that in a few days' time you will be back in Camelot, and I will be alone. I appreciate your offer, but truly, I need to protect myself."

Tristan opened his mouth to refute her but realized that she was right. He nodded, then turned into a horse and walked over to stand next to a tree trunk so Meaghan could mount.

Meaghan took a deep breath, surreptitiously brushed away a few tears, and climbed up on the trunk and then onto Tristan's back. "To the quarry, milord," she said. "And we'd best hurry."

Chapter Forty-two

It was late afternoon when they finally reached the entrance to the quarry. The trees had thinned to small, sparse evergreens, tough enough to survive in the rocky soil. The soil was sandy, and little patches of hardy weeds were scattered around the area. Two huge boulders, taller than Meaghan, stood flanking the narrow path, and looking down the path, she could see other equally large boulders forming the path's wall.

Meaghan slid off Tristan's back and waited until he had assumed his human form. She could see that the time he'd spent as a human had taken its toll. His dark hair was now liberally sprinkled with gray, and the lines around his mouth and his eyes had deepened.

"The quarry is a quarter mile down this road," he explained. "The path to the cave is narrow and runs along the wall of the quarry. I'll be able to traverse the path and get the amulet in a matter of minutes."

"You?" Meaghan asked, shaking her head. "I am quite sure I was told that I needed to obtain the amulet. I will be crossing the path."

She turned away from him and started walking briskly down the narrow path. A moment later she felt his hand on her shoulder, stopping her.

"We haven't finished our discussion," he said tersely.

She looked at him in amazement. "You do realize that a discussion requires two people to converse," she said. "Not just one person telling the other person what's going to happen."

She shrugged his hand off her shoulder and continued forward. A few steps later, she was stopped again. "I won't have you ..."

She looked over her shoulder. "We've had this conversation before too," she said with an impatient sigh. "This is not about you having me do anything."

She continued walking and a few steps later was not only stopped but spun around to face him. She placed her hands on her hips and scowled at him. "The sun is nearly setting," she stated impatiently. "I need to get into the cave and out before the sun sets, so if you would please just allow me to continue…"

"Meaghan, listen to reason," he pleaded.

She held her hand up to stop him. "Fine. Reason," she said. "Do you have a fear of heights?"

He shook his head, completely surprised by her question. "How do you…" he stopped and thought better of his answer. "No."

She nearly smiled. "Tristan, the legend clearly speaks of you climbing Merlin's tower and being afraid of heights," she said. "You must be honest with me."

He sighed. "I am not afraid of anything," he replied and then grudgingly added, "but I do not care for high places with long drops beneath them."

She nodded. "And I have no problem with heights whatsoever," she replied. "And, the Old Mother said that I must retrieve the amulet so it works for me. It will do neither of us any good if the amulet doesn't work for me because you decided to recover it."

"But it could be dangerous," he argued.

She folded her arms over her chest and just stared at him for a long moment. "Truly?" she asked. "Because nothing I have done in the past few days has been dangerous at all."

He sighed. "I am unused to allowing others to put themselves in harm's way while I sit on the side and watch."

She nodded and felt her impatience dissipate. "I can understand that," she said. "But in this quest, you must allow me to complete my tasks. We waste time and energy arguing. You have to trust me."

Nodding, he met her eyes. "Believe me. My arguments have nothing to do with my lack of confidence in you," he said. "Only my desire to keep you safe and protect you."

She smiled at him. "Thank you for that," she said. "And now, what must I do when I enter the cave?"

Chapter Forty-three

Meaghan took a moment to gather her wits before she began the climb across the quarry to the cave entrance. The afternoon sun glared down on the boulders and sandy ground, and the heat was nearly unbearable. She walked to the edge of the quarry pit and looked down, but the glare of the sun made it hard for her to see.

"How deep is it?" she asked Tristan, who was standing a few feet back. She turned and could see that his face was taut with anxiety.

He shook his head. "To be truthful," he explained, "I never came close enough to look."

She nodded. "I'm going to go to the wall to look," she replied. Moving to the side where a tall wall of limestone sheltered one side of the pit, she was finally able to hide from the glare. When she looked down, her stomach lurched.

"What's down there?" Tristan called. "How deep is it?"

She took a deep breath, turned away from the bubbling, orange lava below her and summoned a smile. "It's filled in," she replied. "So, you really can't tell how deep it is."

"Filled in?" Tristan asked. "With water?"

"Yes," she lied, rationalizing there must be some water in that putrid mix. "Exactly. I'm going to start."

The trail to the cave was narrower than the length of Meaghan's foot, not even as wide as the ledges outside the windows of her home. The sheer wall above it had fissures that, she decided, would give her a handhold to keep her balance. And she wouldn't think about the sheer wall below.

Stepping sideways onto the path, she grabbed hold of a tiny crack in the wall and moved forward. The gravel beneath her feet was loose, and she had to step cautiously and secure her foothold before moving on. Sweat slipped down her back as she plastered herself against the rock wall and slowly, painfully moved toward the tiny ledge that held the entrance to the cave. She could smell the noxious fumes being released below and placed her face closer to the wall, hoping fresh air would seep through the gaps.

She was nearly there when the path gave way underneath her foot. She slammed herself against the wall, clutching to the rock with her fingertips to stop her fall. Blindly, she moved her foot forward until she felt solid ground and then tentatively put weight on it.

She shuddered with relief when it held, and she slowly moved forward to the wider out cropping before her.

Reaching the cave entrance, she nearly wept with relief. She placed her hands on her knees and breathed deeply, releasing some of the anxiety she'd felt. She looked over her shoulder and saw that Tristan had turned back into a horse and was pacing back and forth on the other side of the pit. She summoned a cheery wave and then turned back to the black hole before her.

She closed her eyes for a moment, bringing Tristan's instructions to mind.

In the center of the cave, there is a wide path. It is very important that you do not stray to either side of the path. You must stay in the center. When you reach the far end of the cave, there is a small nook in the wall. Reach in and place your hand over the amulet. It will feel like a rock, but it will be smooth. Do not pick up the amulet until it glows brightly and warms in your hand. Then you can pick it up and hurry out of the cave as quickly as possible.

"Why?" she remembered asking him.

He met her eyes. "I only know there are guardians of the amulet," he said, "who may not appreciate its retrieval."

She had nodded, hiding a shiver of fear. "Well, of course, that makes sense," she had tried to respond lightly. "I'll be sure to hurry out."

Now, as she stood in front of the cave, she prayed that the guardians were far away from their amulet and that this retrieval would be fairly simple.

She stepped forward, surprised at how small and narrow the cave entrance was. Then she remembered that those who worked the mine were dwarves. They would have no need for large entrances. She entered, being sure to step in the middle of the path and waited for a moment for her eyes to adjust from the glaring brightness of the rockface to the darkness of the interior of the cave. The inside of the cave opened slightly, but the ceiling was far above her head. The sides of the cave had rust-orange and white water marks, and the ceiling had narrow, twisting stalactites that glowed with pearlescent light. As she moved toward the back, the passageway narrowed so that the walls were an arm's length away from her on either side.

As she continued forward, she lost the light from the entrance and couldn't see anything around her. "How am I supposed to stay on the center of the path when I can't see my hand in front of my face?" she muttered.

She put her hands out to run them along the sides of the wall. "Okay, this works," she said, feeling the rough rock against the tips of her fingertips. Then something slithered over her hand, and she shook her hands rapidly and bit back a scream.

"Okay," she breathed, still cringing. "Not a good idea to touch the side of the cave in the dark."

She moved forward, one hand in front of her, and finally felt another wall. Patting the wall tentatively, she located a hole.

"Please don't be a spider nest," she whispered as she stuck her hand inside the opening. She could feel the strands of spiderwebs tangle against her fingers. She shuddered, but she moved her hand forward. Finally, she touched a cool, smooth object, and with a sigh of relief, she placed her palm over the curved top and let her hand rest on it.

A soft glow began to emanate from the nook, casting a soft light on the area around her. Meaghan could now see that her hand was in an aperture that was manmade with smooth sides and a flat bottom. She looked around and saw the narrow walls were only narrow above her waist. Below, they opened up like a gulley beside the path.

She peered down into the gulley as she kept her hand firmly on the amulet. The light wasn't quite strong enough yet to discern what was down there. She squinted at the objects. Were they small boulders? Were they river stones?

Then the light increased and gave her a clear view. A chill ran down her spine, because the objects she had been staring at were skeletal remains.

Chapter Forty-four

Meaghan looked back at her hand. The glow was brighter, but the stone was still cool to the touch. "Oh, my," she breathed. "You can start to feel warm any time now."

She glanced down at the bones and then back up at her hand. "They're just old bones," she told herself. "They can't hurt me."

Then she felt something hit the side of her foot. She looked down and realized a skull had rolled from the pile of bones. "That's odd…" she began, but then she realized the bones seemed to be shaking.

She swallowed deeply and looked back at the nook. "Hurry. Hurry. Hurry," she urged, glancing back and forth from the shaking bones to her hand.

The shaking continued as the bones started to move around. Meaghan was horrified when the pieces of bones started to move together, reforming into full skeletons. "This cannot be a good thing," she whispered.

She glanced around, looking for any kind of defense, and noticed an old, wooden torch hanging above the nook. She lifted it out of its holder and held it in her other hand. The skeletons shivered and shook as they struggled to acquire an upright stance. A few of them finally stood and stared up at Meaghan with sightless eyes. Then their eyes began to glow red, and they began to chant in a low, rumbling voice, "Aut vincere aut mori."

"Either conquer or die," Meaghan repeated, her voice shaking. "That does not give me much of a choice."

The rest of the skeletons, about fifteen in all, were now standing up, their eyes glowing red, staring at her and chanting. She tightened her hand around the torch and tightened her grip around the amulet. Suddenly, a bright light shot out of the nook, and the amulet was almost too hot to hold.

Pulling her hand and the glowing amulet out of the nook, she screamed as the skeletons started towards her. She lifted the torch and swung it around in a semi-circle, decapitating them and sending their skulls to the ground. Skulls bounced against the path and rolled in every direction. Dropping the torch, Meaghan dashed back down the path. She jumped over the headless skeletons that were madly searching for their heads, and she headed toward the cave entrance.

At the small outcropping in front of the cave, she paused for a moment to catch her breath. She looked across the pit to see Tristan, still a horse, rearing up and pawing at the air.

"I am hurrying," she called across to him. "Believe me."

She shoved the amulet into her pocket and moved back to the narrow ledge. Her heart pounding in her chest, she took a deep breath before she stepped sideways onto the path. She found the handholds and carefully began to pull herself back across the pit.

She had taken no more than four steps when she heard the chanting. Her face plastered against the wall, she couldn't turn around to look. She could only pray that she was faster than they. She moved forward, loose gravel sliding under her feet and down the side of the pit to the lava lake. She clutched to the wall and concentrated on the other side.

Behind her, she could hear the clatter of bone against bone and the sound of gravel being disturbed. They were on the ledge. She heard a quick scurry on loose rock and then heard a deep scream and the clatter of bones against stone. Then she heard the hiss of an object being consumed by the lava.

Shivering with fear, she took another step, her breath coming out in gasps and hitches.

"Come on, darling, you can do it."

She looked ahead to see Tristan, as a man, standing at the edge of the path, his hands outstretched. She met his eyes and felt his strength. "I'm coming," she whispered.

She moved again, and the ledge crumbled behind her. She heard another skeleton fall into the pit below.

"Nearly here," Tristan encouraged. "Only a few more steps."

She stepped again, and her foot slipped to the edge. She screamed and plastered herself against the wall, frozen in fear.

Tristan saw the skeletons, clambering over each other, as they tried to catch up to Meaghan. One of them had nearly made it to the place where the ledge had crumbled. If he made it over, he was only steps away from her.

"Your father would be proud of you," he said.

She looked at him, tears in her eyes, and nodded. "He would want me to try," she said softly, forcing herself to move forward.

Tristan nodded. "He would expect you to do more than try," Tristan said, trying to keep her mind off the skeletons. "He would expect you to conquer."

She smiled and moved again. "Yes, he would," she agreed.

"Come on, only a few more steps," he said and smiled at her. "Then you get to ride."

She felt some of the fear melt away. "I deserve a ride," she replied, moving forward with surer steps.

Tristan saw the skeleton directly behind her reach out its yellowed fingers and try to touch her arm, but she moved forward just as it reached out. With nothing to hold on to, the skeleton lost its footing and dropped into the pit.

Meaghan heard the splash and looked at Tristan with a question in her eyes.

"It was far behind you," he called. "You have them all beat."

She nodded and moved forward. She only had a few more steps to go. Tristan moved closer to the edge and looked down. His stomach dropped, and he nearly stepped back. But when he met Meaghan's eyes, he knew he had to show at least a portion of the courage she had displayed.

"Are you alright?" she asked.

He grinned at her. "I think I'll be fine," he replied, "once you are safely on the ground."

She reached out as she took her final step, and he pulled her into his arms. She went eagerly, burying her face in his chest.

"Meaghan," he whispered. "We have to go."

She looked over her shoulder and saw there were several skeletons nearing the edge of the pit, their eyes glowing and focused on her.

"Yes," she breathed. "Now!"

"Hold on," he cried. He turned around with Meaghan's arms still wrapped around his neck and transformed into a horse, lifting Meaghan onto his back. Meaghan clutched his mane as he thundered away from the pit and down the narrow passageway to the road.

"Will they follow us?" she cried. But before Tristan could respond, the boulders behind them that bordered the path rolled forward, closing off the pathway to the quarry.

When they reached the road, Tristan continued in a gallop until they were several miles away. Then he left the road and stopped in a small, wooded area with a narrow creek. Meaghan slipped off his back and dropped to her knees, splashing her face with water and drinking the cool, clear water.

Tristan transformed and knelt beside her, also drinking his fill. Finally, he sat back and turned to her. "Remind me to never doubt your abilities or your courage," he said softly, caressing her cheek.

She took a deep breath and smiled back. "Remind me to never go into a dark cave again," she said with an involuntary shudder.

He laughed softly. "Aye," he said. "I will."

Chapter Forty-five

Fitz pulled his horse to a halt and slowly looked around the dense woods they had been traveling through. Jepson and Monty stopped beside him and waited silently.

Finally, Fitz turned to the other two men. "We should find shelter for the night," he said. "I have a feeling there is more to this forest than meets the eye."

He urged his horse forward, but before they could follow, Monty reached over and placed his hand on Jepson's arm.

"Yes, milord?" Jepson inquired.

"This fellow, Fitz," Monty said, a quizzical look on his face. "He seems to have a lot of feelings about things. Much more than the average butler. Are we sure that he's quite competent?"

Jepson grinned and nodded. "Yes, milord," he replied. "Fitz is the most competent person we could have in our company. I trust him implicitly."

Monty nodded. "Well, if you say so," he replied. "I've just never met a butler like him before."

Jepson shook his head and started his horse forward into a walk. "There is no butler like him," he said over his shoulder.

With a resigned shrug, Monty followed.

Twenty minutes later, Fitz stopped them again and led them away from the road down a narrow deer path. "As I recall," he mused aloud, "there was a place in these woods…"

He stopped his horse in front of a shallow cave nearly hidden by the ancient trees and smiled. "And I was right," he stated as he dismounted and walked to the cave.

He knelt and felt the ground underneath the layer of dried leaves. "Dry as a desert," he said. "Perfect for a good night's sleep."

Monty dismounted and walked over to him. "But, there's still a few more hours until sundown," he pointed out. "I'm sure we could ride farther."

Fitz turned to him. "We need to set up camp immediately," he replied, not acknowledging Monty's words. "We have no time to lose."

Walking away from Monty, Fitz began to undo the saddle bags on the back of his horse.

"Wait," Monty cried, grabbing Fitz's arm and spinning him around. "I'm the Earl. You need to listen to me."

Fitz stared coldly into Monty's eyes, and Monty immediately dropped his hand and stumbled back. "I mean," Monty stammered. "If you wouldn't mind."

Fitz started to speak, then suddenly glanced up at the sky. "Grab your horse immediately," he shouted, "and bring it into the cave. Now!"

Monty grabbed his horse and pulled him underneath the outcropping of rock. Jepson pulled his horse in alongside Monty's, and Fitz brought his horse in last. "Monty, grab your sword. Jepson, move the horses to the far back of the cave and tether them there," Fitz instructed them. "Then grab your sword and join us."

"Join us for what?" Monty asked, looking up at the sky and only seeing a small flock of birds in the distance. "What's happening?"

"I believe your mother has sent a welcoming party to greet us," Fitz said, staring tensely at the sky.

"Birds?" he asked confused. "Why would she send birds?"

"Not birds," Fitz replied shortly. "Wyverns."

"Wyverns?" Monty asked, watching the flock circle and slowly fly closer to them. Now he could see that what he thought were birds were actually small, winged reptiles with scaled wings and a long tail with an arrow-like tip. "They look like small dragons!"

The black wyvern had a wingspan of about five feet, elongated hind-legs with six-inch claws, and a long tail with a plated tip on the end. Its jaws were long and narrow with razor-sharp teeth, and as it plummeted towards them, it let out a high-pitched, eerie shriek.

Fitz lifted his sword up in a defensive stance. "They are," he cried. "Except their tail and their claws are venomous."

Monty lifted his sword up too as one of the wyverns dove towards him. "How do you kill them?" he shouted.

"Their skin is like plated armor," Fitz said, swinging his sword and frightening one away. "So, it's almost impossible to cut their heads off."

With both hands on his sword, Monty swung hard and hit the side of one of the creatures, sending it sprawling sideways. "What's possible?" he asked.

"Their only vulnerable spot is on their chest," Fitz said. "If you can pierce their chest, you can reach their heart."

"How do you do that without getting stung by their tail?" Monty yelled as he batted another one away.

"With spears," Jepson called, running up to the edge of the cave and looking out to the forest. "We need spears."

"No," Fitz yelled. "We can hold them off."

"There are young rowan trees just a few yards away," Jepson argued. "You keep them occupied, and I'll cut them down."

"No," Fitz yelled. "It's too dangerous."

"Jepson, stop!" Monty called.

But Jepson dashed out of the cave, ignoring their cries. Two of the wyverns saw him and flew in his direction. He sprinted to the forest and dove under a felled tree for protection. The wyverns shrieked and flew up to remount their attack.

Acting quickly, Jepson pulled out his knife and dropped to his knees, chopping the narrow trunk of the tree at an angle so it had a sharp edge. He dropped the first on the ground and moved to the second tree, chopping it as quickly as he could.

One of the wyverns had circled up and was returning for another attack. It flew through the air, it's wings outspread and it's claws forward, ready to rip the flesh of the human it was attacking.

"Jepson, behind you!" Monty screamed.

Jepson grabbed the first trunk and rolled, the trunk pointing up, spearing the beast through it's heart. It shrieked in pain, then convulsed on the edge of the spear and died. Jepson pulled the spear out of the reptile and tossed it to Monty. "I tested it for you," he called. "It works."

Monty grabbed it and from the partial cover of the cave speared another wyvern through it's center. "It works great," he called back to Jepson.

Jepson knelt and finished the work on the second trunk. When he was done, he tossed it to Fitz. "One more," he called to them.

Fitz put his sword down and clasped the sharpened trunk in his hand. He stepped forward, and a wyvern dove at him. He waited until the right time and then thrust the trunk up, catching the creature in the belly. A final shriek and the creature was gone.

Monty smiled at Fitz. "Jepson was right," he said. "We're finally winning."

They had been able to kill nearly all of the wyverns by the time Jepson hacked through the final trunk. He grabbed his trunk and looked back to the cave. The sky was empty, and there were no shrieks to be heard.

"I think you've killed them all," he cried as he sprinted forward.

The final wyvern moved quickly from its hiding place above the cave, its talons spread and deadly. It zeroed in on Jepson, plunging its claws into the flesh above his heart. Jepson screamed and ineffectually tried to drive the creature off with his spear.

Fitz and Monty immediately ran out of the cave.

"Watch for any more," Fitz ordered while he ran to Jepson.

Monty swung his spear around, watching the sky for any other wyverns.

Swinging his spear and fighting the small dragon with all his might, Fitz pounded on its neck and head while the creature mercilessly clawed deeper into Jepson's flesh. Finally, Fitz thrust his spear upwards and drove it through the beast's belly. With a gurgled cry, the beast released Jepson, and Jepson dropped onto his knees, blood flowing from his wound.

Fitz dropped the spear with the beast and knelt next to Jepson to help him stand.

"No, it's too late," Jepson said weakly, shaking his head. He closed his eyes and gasped in pain. "Promise me you'll save Lady Meaghan."

"Yes, I promise," Fitz said softly. "I'll save her."

Jepson opened his eyes, looked into Fitz's eyes and nodded. "I'll let Lord John know…"

Then he closed his eyes, leaned against Fitz and stopped breathing. With tears in his eyes, Fitz slowly lowered Jepson to the ground.

"No!" Monty cried, looking over at them. "No, you have to make him well."

Fitz shook his head. "It's too late," he said hoarsely. "He's gone."

'No, not another one," Monty cried, dropping his spear and kneeling down next to Jepson. "All he wanted was to find Meggie. All he wanted was to help."

"And he did help," Fitz said. "He kept you safe."

Monty brushed his arm over his eyes, wiping away the tears. "He protected me from my mother," he whispered angrily.

"No," Fitz said. "She may have given birth to you, but she was never a mother in the true sense of the word. He protected you from a creature far worse than those we just encountered. And now, we must bury him and be on our way before she realizes her plan did not work."

Chapter Forty-six

Meaghan woke with a start and nearly slipped off Tristan's back. She grabbed onto his mane and gasped in fear. Tristan stopped immediately. "What?" he exclaimed. "What's wrong?"

Her heart pounding, it took a moment for her to be able to speak. "I had a dream," she said with a shudder. "No, a nightmare. I had a nightmare."

"Considering what you went through in the quarry, that's not surprising," Tristan said sympathetically.

She shook her head, feeling calmed by the sound of his voice. "But it wasn't about me," she said. "It was about Jepson."

"Your servant?" Tristan asked.

"My friend," Meaghan replied firmly. "My friend and my father's friend."

"What did you dream?"

"I dreamt that he had died," she said, shivering as she remembered his cries of pain. "It was horrible." She paused for a moment, recalling the details of the dream. "But Fitz was there and Monty, so it couldn't have been real."

"Even so," Tristan said. "Dreams often have messages. What do you think was the message Jepson was sending you?"

"He said he would let my father know," she replied. "Those were his last words. He would let Lord John know."

Tristan, sensing that she was calmer, began to slowly walk down the road again. "What would he let your father know?"

Meaghan shrugged. "I suppose he would let him know that I am carrying on with the task given to our family," she said. "That I would be true to our pledge."

Tristan nodded his head slowly. "That could be what he was saying," Tristan said. "Or he could be letting him know that you are safe, because that would be the first concern of any true parent."

She smiled. "That's a comforting thought," she said softly. "Thank you."

They plodded on in silence for a short while, Meaghan listening to the sounds of the night all around her—the winds whispering gently through the trees, the deeper, haunting sounds of the owls in the trees, the soft scurrying of tiny animals through the leaf beds and the muffled rush of water in the distance. It was almost soothing if she didn't remember that Morganna was out there somewhere planning her demise.

"Can she see us?" Meaghan asked.

"Morganna?" Tristan replied.

"Yes," she said, nodding. "Is there a way for her to see us?"

"She has a scrying bowl," he explained. "Which is like a crystal ball, but it uses water as its medium. But, I believe that as long as you are wearing the amulet, you are hidden from her."

Meaghan smiled and relaxed. "Well, that's good news," she said. "So, we have a little advantage on her. What are our next steps?"

"We should be able to meet the other Eochaidh by morning," he said. "Then we will travel together to the ruin."

"Where is the ruin?" she asked.

"It's on the Isle of Avalon," he said. "A place of old magic and mystery. The ruins were once a castle where Morganna practiced her darkest spells."

"And what are we to do once we get there?" Meaghan asked.

Tristan was silent for a few long moments, and then he sighed. "Well..." he began.

"You don't know," Meaghan interrupted, aghast. "You don't know what we're supposed to do once we get to the ruins? You've had over a thousand years to work this out, and you don't know?"

"Our main focus was finding a Herdin who could help us," Tristan replied defensively. "And now that you're here..."

"Yes?" she asked.

"I guess we'll figure it out," he said. "We have all the right ingredients; the pieces are sure to fall into place."

"I don't think that's a strategy most great leaders follow," she quipped.

He stopped and looked back at her. "It's called faith," he said. "We did our part. We did all we could. Now the rest has to fall into place."

Meaghan shook her head. "I don't know if I have any faith left," she admitted. "But I have a sense of duty. So, perhaps that will be enough."

Chapter Forty~seven

"We need to stop for the night," Tristan said after they'd traveled for another hour.

Meaghan shook her head and tried not to yawn. "I'm fine," she said. "I can go on."

"You've nearly slipped from my back several times," he said. "And once we leave this forest, we'll be traveling across mountains and bluffs. A slip then could be deadly."

"I'll stay awake," she insisted.

He left the road and walked down a narrow path to a small, concealed grove. "Then you'll be walking on your own," he said. "I'm stopping for the night."

She slid off his back, and although she loathed to admit it, it felt good to stop and stretch.

"There's bread and cheese in the saddlebags," Tristan said.

"But what about you?" Meaghan asked.

"As long as I stay a horse, this grass will suffice," he said.

She smiled. "I suppose there are advantages to being a horse," she said.

He shook his head. "Aye, but I am anxious for the day when I put these four legs behind me," he admitted.

Hearing the sound of water close by, she turned and could see a small brook just beyond the grove. "I'm going to wash up," she said. "I'll only be a moment."

Tristan looked over to see the proximity of the brook and then nodded. "Don't take too long," he said, and then began to nibble on a tall patch of grass.

Meaghan wound her way through the dense trees, stepping over large rocks and downed tree trunks, and finally came to the brook. She stepped to the edge of the bank and realized that it was a four-foot drop to the water. "That's not going to work," she muttered.

She looked up and down the brook for a place where the bank might angle down gradually but

274

could see nothing in the area. With a sigh, she grabbed hold of a young sapling and started to lower herself down the side. She was nearly to the bottom when the sapling snapped, and she fell backwards, landing on her back with a thump. The amulet, that she'd been carrying in her pocket, slipped out and rolled several feet away. "Well, that was graceful," she muttered, picking herself up and walking toward the amulet.

Lady Strathmore sat in her sitting room, angrily tapping a long, blood-red fingernail on the side of the silver bowl. She had cast the spell to search for Lady Meaghan, and all she saw in the bowl was a fine mist. "She's out there," she growled. "I know she's out there."

Suddenly, the mist cleared, and Lady Strathmore could see Meaghan lying in the sand alongside a brook. She watched her get up and walk toward the water, and then the mist appeared once again.

"I know that place," Lady Strathmore exclaimed. "She's only a quarter-day's ride to the ruins."

She jumped up and ran across the room, pulling the double doors open with violent force. "Get my carriage and team ready," she shouted. "We are leaving at once."

Chapter Forty-eight

Hours later, Tristan lifted his head and looked down at Meaghan. She was lying against his side, her head resting on his shoulder, and she was sound asleep. He studied her face, relaxed and peaceful.

"What are you dreaming about, my love?" he whispered.

She smiled in her sleep and nestled closer to him. His heart ached at the injustice of life. He'd finally found the only woman he would ever love, and by tomorrow, she would be a thousand years away from him. But he had tonight, he reminded himself. If nothing else, he had this short respite from danger to make a memory that would have to last him the rest of his life.

He changed from horse to man and gathered Meaghan into his arms. She sighed softly and buried her face against his neck. He closed his eyes with the sweetness of her movements and placed a kiss on the top of her head. He inhaled her scent, committing it to memory. He stroked her hair, fingering the silken tresses, soothing not only the woman in his arms but himself as well.

There was no thought of carnal pleasures. There was only a desire to protect, cherish, and love. He closed his eyes and felt the sweet anguish in his soul. To love so deeply and know that it could never be realized. To know that, once you left, you would leave the love of your life defenseless and bereft. What kind of cruel trick had fate played on both of them?

She whispered his name in her sleep, soft and soothing.

"Meaghan," he whispered. "I will love you forever."

She sighed and murmured softly, but although he tried, he couldn't hear what she said. Shaking his head, he smiled sadly. "Sleep, my love, for the morrow will bring us joy and sadness."

Then he closed his eyes and fell asleep too.

The sun was barely peaking over the horizon when Meaghan awoke. She felt warm and safe, and more rested than she had in a long time. She tried to move but realized her arms were caught tightly against her body. Immediately, she remembered the roots and began to panic, but then she felt the steady heartbeat thrumming against her own. Her mind clearing, and her vision focused, she realized she was wrapped in Tristan's arms.

An unbridled thrill swept through her body as she lay against him, feeling his breath against her hair. She relaxed, enjoying this stolen moment of tenderness. She inhaled his scent and knew that she would remember it always. She felt the strength of his arms and knew no other arms would ever hold her with such care. And she knew, deep in her heart, that she would never love another as she did him.

He shifted slightly, and his hold loosened. Carefully, she slipped out from within his arms. She knelt beside him for a moment, watching him sleep, feeling an overwhelming urge to run her fingers through his hair and brush his wayward locks away from his face. But she fought the urge, knowing that it might wake him. He needed his rest for the day ahead.

She slipped silently to her feet and walked over to their supplies, placing her scabbard and sword on underneath her shirt. Then she stole into the forest to see to her morning ablutions. The day was already warm, and the birds were beginning their morning chorus. She could still hear the final stanzas of the tree frogs and toads echoing in the woods as Meaghan moved closer to the brook. She carefully climbed down and splashed cold water on her face. She took several minutes to wash up and make herself ready for the long ride ahead.

She had turned to climb back up onto the bank when she heard a sound from across the brook. She paused and listened intently.

"Meaghan! Meaghan!"

Who could be calling her name?

A few flat stones created a walkway across the brook, and Meaghan nimbly crossed over to the other side. The bank was gentler here and rose to a meadow filled with spring flowers. She climbed up, walked to the meadow and slowly searched the area.

"Meaghan!"

She turned toward the voice and gasped aloud. "Mother," she screamed, running through the field towards the woman on the other side. "Mother, I thought you had died."

The woman waved to her and began to slowly walk towards her. "Meaghan," she called out, her voice filled with delight. "I've finally found you."

"Mother," Meaghan cried, tears flowing down her face. "Oh, I'm…"

She stopped suddenly, her heart pounding in her chest. There was something wrong; she could feel it. She stepped backwards. "How did you know I was here?" she asked.

"Does it really matter, my dear?" the woman asked. "All that matters is that we are together."

Meaghan shook her head. "You're not my mother," she said angrily.

The vision of her mother faded, and Lady Strathmore took its place. "No, you are quite right," Lady Strathmore said. "How clever of you, Lady Meaghan. But, unfortunately, you didn't figure that out until you were well within my grasp."

She lifted her arms, whispered a spell, and then pointed her hands in Meaghan's direction.

Meaghan stood her ground, reaching surreptitiously for her sword.

"It didn't harm you!" Lady Strathmore cried, incensed.

Meaghan shrugged. "Not quite as powerful as you thought," she quipped.

Lady Strathmore's eyes narrowed, and she glared at Meaghan. "Perhaps we just need to change venues," she snarled. Once again, she lifted her hands to the skies, and a small, dark cloud appeared above her, circling ominously above both of them.

Lady Strathmore smiled at Meaghan, and the madness in her eyes caused Meaghan to shudder.

"I understand you wanted to visit the ruins," Lady Strathmore seethed. "Well, allow me to help you on your journey."

The cloud dropped, encompassing them both, and Meaghan was swept away in the maelstrom of the wind. The ground below her grew farther away. She could see Tristan moving around the meadow in search of her. She tried to call to him, but her words were whipped away by the force of the tempest. Then, suddenly they were moving across country. She held onto her sword with one hand and the amulet with the other to be sure they weren't whipped away.

Finally, the cloud began to dissipate, and Meaghan felt herself falling from the sky. She looked down and saw huge towers of rock forming a circle in the middle of a field below her. She wondered how it would feel to crash against one of the rocks, if her death would be sudden or slow and painful.

Then the speed of her descent lessened until she was floating down like a feather in the wind. She landed softly on her feet in the middle of the stone circle. And, a moment later, Lady Strathmore landed several yards away.

"I do not know what magic you command," Lady Strathmore screamed. "But it will be useless against my sword."

Chapter Forty-nine

Tristan awoke with a start. His muscles ached, and his body felt weary. It took him a moment to remember where he was. Then he looked down at the imprint on the ground beside him and remembered, with a smile, that he had spent the night with Meaghan secure in his arms. It only took a moment longer for disquiet to enter his thoughts. He sat up and glanced around.

"Meaghan," he called out. "Meaghan, where are you?"

He stood and immediately felt the toll the hours as a man had cost him as his body responded slowly. He hurried to the edge of the clearing. "Meaghan?" he called out, a note of panic now entering his voice. "Where are you?"

He hurried into the forest and noted the path in the dew-swept grass. She had been down this way, he reasoned. She was probably safe. He hurried forward toward the small brook and saw her crossing the water.

"Meaghan," he yelled. "Meaghan come back."

She seemed focused on something across the brook and, once on the other side, continued into the meadow.

"Meaghan!" he screamed. He was running now, with branches and brush scraping against his face as he barreled through the woods. "Meaghan!"

He slipped down the embankment, barely staying on his feet, and then splashed through the brook. He looked up, gasping for breath, and saw that she'd stopped.

"Meaghan!" he cried again and then ran forward.

Suddenly a cloud descended on her and lifted her into the sky. "No!" he screamed, helpless as he watched her ascend into the air. His heart dropped in fear. Meaghan was now in the hands of Morganna.

He immediately turned back into a horse and galloped across the meadow, following the direction of the cloud. He had to find her, had to reach her, before Morganna disposed of the last Herdin.

Pounding across the meadow, his large hooves throwing up clumps of grass and dirt behind him, he made his way towards the road. There were only three miles between their campsite and the ruins, and he was sure Morganna was taking Meaghan there. He jumped over the small, stone fence at the edge of the meadow, landed solidly on the dirt road and charged forward, putting everything he had into maintaining his speed.

With his long gait, he ate up the road quickly, scattering pebbles and dust as he galloped forward. His breath was even and steady, his pace solid and rapid, and his sole focus was the Isle of Avalon.

Too late he realized he was at a crossroads, and two riders were entering the road just ahead of him. He knew that he would not be able to stop before he collided with them, so he gathered up his strength and jumped. He cleared the first rider, who had screamed in fear and ducked down in the saddle. But the second rider, an older man, was not as quick, and Tristan caught his shoulder with his back hoof, knocking the man from his horse onto the road.

With more than a little regret, Tristan knew that he didn't have time to stop for the man. His main concern was getting to Meaghan as quickly as possible. So, with only a backward glance of regret, he continued.

"Stop!"

The command seemed to echo all around Tristan, and he found, to his surprise, that he was frozen in place.

"What devilment is this?" he shouted.

The old man stood and peered at Tristan. "Tristan?" he asked, amazed.

Tristan found he could turn his head and looked back at the man he'd knocked over.

"Merlin?" he asked, aghast.

"Merlin?" Monty repeated, equally as surprised.

Fitz sighed and nodded. "Yes, I am Merlin."

Chapter Fifty

Once Fitz had remounted his horse and Tristan had explained the urgency of his mission, they immediately set forward together, galloping down the road towards the island.

Monty had nearly been left behind as he stared in shocked silence at the giant horse carrying on a conversation with the infamous wizard. It took him several seconds of stunned stupor to realize that they were leaving him in their dust. Urging his steed on, he caught up with the others, and they rode neck and neck together.

Finally, Monty found his voice and turned to his friend's old retainer. "Are you really Merlin?" he shouted over to the older man.

Fitz nodded. "Yes, milord, I am," he replied.

"Then why are you working as a butler, of all things?" he asked. "A bit down on your luck?"

Fitz bit back a smile and shook his head. "No, actually, my fortune is fine," he replied. "But I wanted to be available to help the Herdin family defeat Morganna."

"Well, from my point of view," Monty said, "you certainly made a mess of things—most of the Herdin family dead and Meaghan in Morganna's clutches. Maybe the legends just made you out to be better than you really were."

Fitz glanced over at Monty, his jaw set in anger. "Young man, if you would like a quick demonstration of my abilities, I would be more than happy to oblige."

Monty shook his head. "No offense meant," Monty quickly replied. "But, it just seems that if you have an all-powerful wizard on your side, things shouldn't be so hard."

"Even wizards are limited in what they can do," Fitz said.

They rode for several more minutes as Monty thought about Fitz's answer. He could smell the sea in the air as they got closer. The tide was low, and the sandbar was visible from the road. Tristan, leading the way, charged from the road across the beach to the sandbar and flew across the wet sand to the island beyond.

Fitz and Monty followed, their horses not as sure-footed on the wet sand, so they had to slow their pace.

"Lady Strathmore, my mother," Monty finally said. "Or, Morganna, whoever she is. She didn't seem to have any limitations. She created chaos, murdered people, and ruined lives. But she seems to go about her life willy-nilly, with no thought to repercussions."

Fitz was silent for a moment. Then he turned to the young man. "She has no thought for repercussions because she is consumed by jealousy and power. She does not look at the cost. She only looks at what she perceives is the final outcome."

"The final outcome?" Monty asked, his tone bitter. "How could all of this benefit her?"

"Revenge against Arthur," Fitz said simply. "She has wasted her life, sacrificed her soul and destroyed herself because she desired revenge."

"Did he treat her so poorly this was justified?" Monty asked.

Fitz shook his head. "He was not perfect, by no means," he explained. "But his sin against her was more in her mind than in reality. Had she just taken a moment to reason..." He sighed. "Well, we would not be where we are today."

Chapter Fifty-one

Meaghan placed her hand on the hilt of her sword and felt it warming to her touch. Amazed, she pulled it out of the scabbard and held it up. The silver metal of the sword was glowing a soft blue, and the energy was pulsing from the weapon into Meaghan's arm, giving her a feeling of strength and power.

She looked up at Morganna, who was slowly advancing towards her, and positioned herself to fence. She intuitively knew that she needed to come from a position of defense, not aggression, to have the magic work for her.

"I would ask you to throw down your sword," Meaghan stated firmly. "And begin negotiations for your punishment."

Morganna stopped in her tracks and looked at Meaghan in astonishment. "You do realize that you are about to die, do you not?" she asked. "Are you trying to act mad in order to gain my sympathy?"

Meaghan shook her head. "You have tried to kill me several times," she replied more confidently than she felt. "And, as you can see, I am still here. However, I have not tried to kill you, yet. It would seem the odds favor me."

Morganna curled her lip in disdain. "I am not your father, playing swords with a child," she sneered.

Meaghan took a quick breath and could feel anger flowing through her veins. Then, she could hear her father's voice in her mind. *Careful, Meggie. Don't let her distract you with emotion. Be cool. Be calm. Be the warrior I know you are.*

Breathing in again, she relaxed and smiled. "I believe you misunderstood the relationship," she said sweetly. "'Twas I who was easy on him."

Morganna lunged forward, and Meaghan easily countered, knocking Morganna back several feet. "I will give you one more chance to surrender," Meaghan said, her eyes blazing with determination. "And that will be all."

She nearly smiled when she saw the particle of doubt light in Morganna's eyes. Then it was replaced by rage.

Good, Meaghan thought. *Let emotion distract you.*

"Who do you think you are to command me so?" Morganna spat.

"Merely your better," Meaghan replied easily.

"You bitch!" Morganna screamed, running at Meaghan.

Meaghan waited until the sorceress was nearly upon her. Then she twisted sideways and parried Morganna's blade, pushing it to the side. Meaghan quickly lunged forward and slashed Morganna's hand, leaving a line of red behind.

Morganna stumbled back and repositioned herself. Meaghan held her ground and waited.

"I underestimated you," Morganna scoffed. "You are much more masculine than I would have guessed."

Meaghan nodded. "And up close, you look far older than I had imagined," she replied easily.

She watched Morganna's eyes widen and waited for the attack. It was not long in coming. But this time, the rage caused Morganna to forgo the basic rules of swordplay and come out swinging like a madman—a far more dangerous situation for Meaghan

Stepping back to reposition herself, Meaghan put both hands on her hilt and held it up in a defensive position. As Morganna came closer, Meaghan attacked, meeting her sword blow for blow, feeling the force vibrate through her arms and the clanging echo in her ears. For every wild thrust, Meaghan was able to parry and riposte, but no one was gaining ground.

Suddenly, Meaghan remembered one of her favorite ploys with her father. She allowed Morganna's sword to glance over her shoulder, and she gasped in mock pain. The sound brought a triumphant glitter into Morganna's eyes, and she paused in her attack for just a moment. But a moment was all Meaghan needed. She parried with all of her might and knocked Morganna's sword out of her hands.

Moving in for the final thrust, Meaghan heard Monty call out. She turned, distracted for a moment. Morganna thrust out her hand towards her sword, and the sword flew back to her.

Meggie! Her father's voice screamed in her mind.

She turned just in time to see Morganna's sword bearing down on her.

Chapter Fifty-two

Meaghan didn't know if it was instinct or the magic embedded in the sword, but without conscious thought, she brought her sword forward and blocked Morganna's nearly fatal thrust. She jumped back and positioned herself in a defensive stance.

"You fool!" Fitz whispered harshly, grabbing Monty by the collar and pulling him behind a stone. "Are you trying to get her killed?"

"I'm sorry," Monty stammered. "I didn't think. I just saw her standing there and…"

"And you distracted her," Tristan said, pulling his own sword out and holding it to Monty's throat. He looked at Fitz. "Are you certain this one is not in league with Morganna?"

Monty, his eyes wide with horror, stared at Tristan. "Who's he?" he asked Fitz. "Where did he come from?"

"He's the horse," Fitz said. "He's one of the Eochaidh." Fitz turned to Tristan and shook his head. "No, he's not in league with her, I can assure you.

He's been Meaghan's lifelong friend and was merely happy to see her."

Tristan lowered his sword. "Friend or not, you endanger her life again, and I will kill you."

Standing next to the large stones, Tristan carefully moved forward, trying to inch his way in without detection. Meaghan was more than holding her own in the battle, but he wanted to ensure her safety. However, as he tried to step into the inner circle, his way was blocked by some invisible force. He tried another direction. Once again he was unable to enter. He backed out and turned to Fitz. "I cannot enter," he growled softly. "You must help me get in."

Fitz shook his head. "The magic that bars your way is much older than I am and much stronger," he said. "We will not be allowed to enter until their contest is completed."

Fitz walked over and peered into the stone circle, watching Meaghan advance on Morganna and causing her to retreat. He turned to Tristan. "That is not her sword," he said. "Where did she get that?"

Tristan came over to Fitz's side. "You're right. Her own sword remains on her saddle," he said. "She must have received it from the little man."

"Little man?" Fitz asked, his eyebrows raised in wonder.

"A group of thugs were able to steal me from Meaghan and brought me into town," he said. "On her way into town, she was met by a little man, one of the fae, who gave her a gown to wear to trick the men. She said he was a collector."

"Is that so?" Fitz replied, peering once again at the sword and smiling. "That sword has found her way home. It came from Avalon and is a sister sword to Excalibur. Meaghan has a true ally in that weapon."

Monty cautiously joined the men, watching over their shoulders. "Is there nothing we can do to help her?" he whispered.

"We can be quiet and not distract her," Fitz replied quietly but firmly.

Suddenly, the sound of horses came from behind them. Tristan turned, his sword at the ready, and then, when he saw it was the other Eochaidh, he dropped it and hurried forward to meet them.

"Meaghan's fighting Morganna," he whispered urgently. "We must not distract her."

"We need to help her," Sir Garrett replied, changing to a man and brandishing his sword.

Tristan shook his head. "We cannot; the way is blocked," he said. "All we can do is watch."

"Aye, and pray," Rufus said, changing to a man and walking up to the stones to watch the battle.

Andrew and Duncan also changed to men and hurried to join the others at the stone circle.

"Who are these men?" Monty whispered urgently.

"They are knights of Arthur's Round Table," Fitz replied, "who were cursed by your mother."

"The Eochaidh are real," Monty said, shaking his head in wonder. "I always thought they were a faery tale."

"Faery tales are often more real than we care to believe," Fitz said, watching the women battle. "And more dangerous."

Chapter Fifty-three

Meaghan could feel herself tiring. With every parry and riposte, she could feel her strength ebb away and her nimbleness lessen. She was heartened to see that Morganna seemed to be fatiguing too. At this point, they were so evenly matched the fight could last for hours. But she knew she had to somehow gain the advantage over Morganna and soon.

She noticed the sun was just cresting over the stones at the far end of the circle. Once they did, Morganna would have the advantage because the sun would be in Meaghan's eyes. But, Meaghan thought with a smile, not if she harnessed its rays first.

She slowly retreated several feet to a slight rise in the ground, placing her at a slightly higher elevation than Morganna. The sorceress followed her, swinging her blade with determination and anger. "I will destroy you," she gasped as sweat glistened on her brow.

Meaghan took a deep breath and nodded at her. "Not if I destroy you first," she said.

Morganna swung her sword sideways, and Meaghan countered, angling her blade so it not only caught Morganna's blade flatly on its side but also caught the bright beam of the sun as it came over the top of the stone. The reflection blinded Morganna, and she stumbled back. Meaghan swung with all of her might, hitting Morganna's sword and knocking it from her hand. Then she continued her attack, cutting Morganna's arm with her sword.

Morganna clutched her sword arm with her other hand to staunch the flow of blood. "This is not over!" she screamed.

"Meaghan, the amulet," Sir Garrett cried.

Meaghan raised her sword and lifted it next to Morganna's neck, catching the leather cord that held the blood amulet. The cord severed, and the amulet fell onto the ground.

Morganna tried to retrieve it, but Meaghan stepped forward and held her sword to Morganna's throat. "I think it's time for you to surrender," Meaghan said.

Morganna, her eyes blazing with hate, stared at Meaghan for a long moment. "I will see you in hell first!" she screamed. She lifted her arms, and a swirling portal appeared behind her. With a triumphant smile, she stepped backwards into it. "This is not over."

The portal closed, and Morganna was gone.

Meaghan stood staring at the portal for a long moment and then dropped to her knees in exhaustion. She dropped her sword, placed her hands on her thighs, and bent her head, drawing in long draughts of cool air.

"You were magnificent."

She looked up to Tristan and smiled. "Thank you, milord," she replied softly. Then she looked beyond him and gasped. "Fitz? Fitz, you're alive?"

She scrambled to her feet and ran to him, throwing her arms around his waist.

"How did you? How long?" she stammered.

"He's not just Fitz," Monty interjected. "He's Merlin. You know, the wizard."

Meaghan stumbled backwards and stared at him. "Merlin?" she asked.

He nodded slowly. "Yes, I am," he said. Then he sent an angry glare in Monty's direction. "Although I would have preferred to tell you in my own way."

"But then...you could have saved them," she said, shaking her head in confusion. "You could have stopped her."

"No, my dear," he replied softly. "I did all I could do. Morganna's powers..."

"No!" Meaghan shouted as tears of anger and frustration slipped down her cheeks. "Do not tell me that her powers were too strong. I just beat her. I just beat the amazing Morganna. I am not a wizard or even a knight of the Round Table. Why couldn't you stop her?"

Fitz sighed. "Because we weren't meant to stop her," he said. "You were."

"My parents were meant to die?" she asked, her voice breaking. "They were good people who never hurt anyone."

He nodded. "They were exceptionally good people," he agreed, "who did not deserve what Morganna did to them. And you did not deserve to have this thrust upon you. But this life does not always give us what we deserve, only what is meant to be."

"And who decides what is meant to be?" Meaghan countered. "Do you? Does Morganna? Does the fate of my family lie in something that happened thousands of years ago?"

Fitz studied her for a moment and then gently asked, "Who decided that you should go on this quest?"

She closed her eyes for a moment and took a shuddering breath. Then she opened them and looked at him. "I did," she said. "I decided."

He nodded. "And who decided to stay at the estate in Wales and train his daughter to be a warrior?" he asked.

She sighed deeply. "My father."

He shook his head. "Both your father and your mother," he replied. "They were in total agreement. They could have gone to London and relinquished their part in this quest."

"No, they couldn't have," she replied sadly. "Because they were people of honor."

"Yes, they were," Fitz replied. "Better people I have never met."

Wiping a stray tear from her cheek, she shook her head. "But that doesn't matter," she said, "because they're gone."

He stepped forward, put his hand on her shoulder and met her eyes. "Are they gone, Meaghan?" he asked. "Are they truly gone?"

She thought back to the fight—thought back to her father's words so clear in her mind—and shook her head. "But where are they?" she asked.

He smiled sadly. "And that is a question that even the greatest wizard cannot answer with certainty," he said. "But I know it is a matter of faith and acceptance. That's why they made the choices they made; they had faith that there was more than just this life. And they knew that they would never truly be separated from you."

Chapter Fifty-four

It was a quiet and solemn procession that walked from the stone circle to the ruins on the top of the nearby hill, each person lost in their own thoughts. They climbed the crumbling stone steps and walked through the remnants of the archway that led to the main chamber of the castle. Grass grew where a stone floor had once lay. Four towering, partially-derelict, stone walls stood surrounding them, and the only ceiling above was the blue sky.

In the middle of the chamber was a large stone with a flattened surface. It was scarred where edges of blades and axes had been embedded in its surface, and it was stained with the blood of thousands of years of conflict.

"This is not a good place," Meaghan said, shivering as she stood next to the dark stone.

"At one time it was," Fitz explained. "But it always was a place of power. And, unfortunately, power often has a way of attracting the unsavory and evil personalities of humankind. Too many people have died here. Too many people have realized that power, for power's sake, is an empty promise."

"What must we do here?" Tristan asked.

"Reverse the spell she placed on you," Fitz said. "And then return to Camelot to prevent this from happening again."

"This is it?" Rufus asked. "This is all there is to it?"

"Well, I do have to concoct the potion," Fitz said. "What did you want to happen?"

Rufus shrugged. "Well, I suppose I thought there would be a great battle," he said. "A war of good against evil."

"I thought we witnessed that this morning," Garrett inserted, examining the amulet he had picked up from the ground after the sword fight. "Lady Meaghan was the champion for us all."

"Aye, the lass was truly amazing," Rufus agreed. "But, I thought there would be more for the rest of us to do."

"You discount so easily the battles all of you have endured," Fitz said. "Lady Meaghan giving up anger and revenge for duty. You knights giving up safety, security and family to serve your king and your country. Even young Monty here, sacrificing comfort and home to help his friend. Each of you have fought battles of the heart, which, in my opinion, are often greater than those on the field."

Rufus shrugged. "Just thought I'd be able to use my sword more," he mumbled.

Fitz chuckled softly and then looked out over the east wall. "We must catch the sun at the correct position, so we need to start now."

He unpacked his saddle bag and placed a wide, shallow bowl made of wood on the stone. Then he pulled out a number of small, amber bottles, each labeled in Latin and sealed with a cork. He opened each one and poured out a measured amount. Then he pulled several small, leather pouches from his bag. He took a pinch of each and sprinkled them on top of the liquid. He stepped back and nodded with satisfaction. "And now, Lady Meaghan, if I may have your hand," he said.

Tristan stepped forward, blocking Meaghan. "What are you going to do to her?" Tristan asked.

Fitz smiled. "I merely need a drop of her blood," he said. "A mere prick of my knife's tip on her finger."

Tristan turned to Meaghan. "You don't have to…"

She smiled at him. "It will be fine," she said, offering her hand to Fitz.

He gently pushed the tip of his knife into her fingertip until a drop of blood appeared. Then he squeezed her finger until her blood dropped onto the liquid in the bowl.

"And now," Fitz said. "The thing Morganna holds dear to her."

Sir Garrett pulled the amulet out of his pocket and handed it to Fitz. "Is this it?" he asked. "The last item for the potion?"

Fitz nodded. "Yes, this will create the potion to break the spell."

Sir Garrett nodded. "It's hard to believe it's almost over," he said, his voice thick with emotion. "It's hard to believe we are going home."

Fitz dropped the amulet into the potion and waited, but nothing happened.

"Is something supposed to happen?" Meaghan asked.

Fitz nodded. "Yes, something is supposed to happen," he said slowly. "But unfortunately, nothing is."

"Was it my blood?" Meaghan asked, her eyes wide with regret.

"Blood," Fitz replied with a nod. "I believe—"

"All this way for naught," Morganna cackled as she stepped out of a portal at the corner of the room. "But how lucky for me that I have all the people I want to destroy gathered together in one room."

Chapter Fifty-five

The knights ran forward, their swords poised for battle, and created a barrier between Morganna and the others.

"Take this bowl and hide," Fitz said, handing the bowl with the potion to Meaghan. He turned to Monty. "Protect her and the spell."

Meaghan looked around the room and saw the remains of an old staircase adjacent to the wall. "Over there," she whispered to Monty.

He looked at the staircase and shook his head. "You'll die trying to climb up it," he said.

"I don't want to climb up it," she said. "I want to hide the bowl underneath it."

"Oh! Good plan," he replied. He began to hurry with her to the other side of the room when he saw a shadow streak across the far wall. He turned and watched in horror as a flock of wyverns flew from the portal into the ruin.

"Run, Meggie!" he cried, pushing her on her way. "Hide under the stairway."

She looked at the small dragons and gasped. "What are they?"

"They're deadly," he shouted. "Now go!"

She started to move then stopped when she realized he was running for the archway. "Where are you going?" she yelled.

"To get my spear," he called back.

Meaghan dashed ahead and pushed herself into a small fissure underneath the stone staircase. She felt around in the darkness and discovered a place where a stone had fallen out of the wall. It was just deep enough for her to securely slip the bowl inside. Once the potion was secure, she slipped back out of the opening and reached for her sword. A black wyvern came screeching towards her, its talons outstretched. Meaghan felt the power of the sword thrum in her hand as she swept it forward. The blue light of the blade seemed to sparkle with power, and she thrust it into the wyvern's neck. The creature exploded into ash.

"Wow! Meggie, that was incredible," Monty said, his spear in his hand. "But you have to be careful. Their feet and their tails have venom."

Meaghan looked at the long, pointed shaft Monty was carrying. "Where did you get that?" she asked, a little amused at her friend's weapon.

Monty clasped it with both hands, readying for a thrust, and turned to her. "Jepson made it for me before he died."

Meaghan felt as if she'd been speared. "Jepson's dead?" she whispered, leaning back against the wall.

But Monty didn't hear her as he moved forward with purpose, dashing forward and spearing the wyverns.

Meaghan wiped the tears from her eyes and took a deep breath. She could mourn later. Now she had to fight.

She too ran forward, slashing her blade through the air and connecting with the dragons.

Tristan stood on top of the stone table, slashing and thrusting his sword into the flock. It took both of his hands and all of his strength to wield his broadsword effectively, as he felt the effects of his advancing years. A wyvern attacked from the side, and Tristan stumbled, nearly falling off the table, but instead dropped to one knee. The wyvern dove again, its talons outstretched, he struggled to lift his sword in defense. He could see the razorlike claws descended toward his face and braced for the impact when the creature burst into ashes inches from his face.

He turned to see Monty standing next to him, pulling back his spear and readying himself for another target.

"My thanks," Tristan breathed, getting to his feet.

Monty shrugged. "I'm not going to let these things kill any more of my friends."

Tristan smiled at the young man and nodded. "I'm honored to be your friend."

Monty pivoted and thrust his spear into another dragon, so it too burst into ashes. Then he turned back to Tristan with a smile on his face. "I'm honored too," he said.

"If it's all the same to you two friends," Rufus called from his position next to the portal. "If we could concentrate on killing the wee dragons instead of chit-chat, I'd be grateful."

Rufus swung his sword in a great arch and cut off the heads of three of the creatures as they flew into the room.

"I thought you said you wanted to use your sword more," Tristan replied, stabbing another one through the heart.

"Aye, so I did," Rufus admitted, turning and catching another that was attacking from behind him. "Remind me to shut my mouth next time."

A half-dozen wyverns targeted Duncan and Andrew and the two knights, fought them fiercely, moving back as they swung and slashed the creatures. But the creatures kept at them, forcing them back into a corner of two of the stone walls. In the small space, their movements were limited, and they found themselves only able to stab at the creatures.

"We could use a little assistance here," Duncan cried out, ducking when one nearly caught the top of his head.

"I'm coming," Monty cried, jumping across the room and spearing two at one time.

Garrett stepped into the fray and killed two others, so Duncan and Andrew could move about freely.

"My thanks," Duncan said to Monty. "Well done."

But before another word could be spoken, more of the creatures came flying through the portal at them.

With his sword in his hand, Fitz quietly sought Morganna and the portal. His back plastered against the wall, he moved within the shadows and soundlessly rounded the corner, so he was next to the swirling vortex. Whispering quietly, he closed his eyes and summoned his power. His sword began to glow, but he waited, watching the melee in front of him. Finally, when his sword was blazing, he jumped forward and slashed through the wall of the portal.

Instantly, the vortex began to rock crookedly off its base. The wyverns flew into the edges of the portal and were knocked backwards. Morganna screamed and jumped forward into the room as the portal closed with a burst of light. She fell onto her knees and quickly picked herself up, lifting her sword in front of her.

The small flock of wyverns was nearly destroyed, but the last one hurled itself at Meaghan with brutal purpose. Meaghan screamed as the talons clamped down on her shoulder, but before it could break the skin and poison her, she brought her sword up to impale it. The creature shattered into the air.

But, Monty only heard her scream. "Meggie!" Monty yelled, blindly rushing forward with his spear with no thought to his own safety. When he ran past Morganna, she lifted her sword over her head and thrust it into his back.

He dropped his spear and froze in his steps. Blood ran from his lips, and his eyes widened in shock. "Meggie," he whispered, and then he collapsed onto the ground.

"No!" Meaghan cried, and she threw her own sword across the room, her aim sure and strong. It glowed in the dimness of the ruin and found its objective in Morganna's heart.

Chapter Fifty-six

Like ancient parchment that had been set to fire, Morganna's body crumpled into itself, curling and folding toward the sword projecting from the middle of her body. Finally, her remains were only dark ashes that were swept away by the wind, and the sword clattered to the floor.

Meaghan rushed over to Monty and knelt by his side, cradling his head in her lap. She brushed his hair tenderly from his face and stroked his cheek. He opened his eyes and tried to smile at her.

"Are you alright?" he asked.

She nodded, tears running down her face. "Yes," she whispered. "You saved me."

"I did, didn't I?" he replied with a weak grin. "I was brave, wasn't I?"

"You were so brave," she agreed.

"I'm not like her," he insisted, his voice softer.

"No," Meaghan agreed. "You are not like her at all. You are good and brave and noble. My father would have been so proud of you."

He sighed softly and nodded. "Thank you, Meggie."

Then he closed his eyes and shuddered his last breath. Sobbing uncontrollably, she bent over and hugged him to her. "I'm so sorry, Monty," she whispered. "I'm so sorry."

"Lady Meaghan."

Meaghan looked up, her eyes red and swollen, her face awash with tears, and faced Fitz. "Can I not grieve for my friend?"

His eyes filled with regret, he shook his head. "Morganna is not dead," he said gently. "Because she does not belong to this time, she was merely transported back to Camelot. We must break the spell and go back for her."

She wiped her sleeve across her face to blot the tears and nodded, gently easing Monty's body tenderly onto the ground. "What would you have me do?" she asked wearily.

"I need you to retrieve the potion," he said, and then he glanced up at the sky. "And we only have minutes to complete the spell."

Meaghan stood and hurried to the staircase, retrieved the bowl from the hole in the wall and brought it to the stone table. "It didn't work last time," she said. "What can we do that's different?"

Fitz held up a small vial containing dark red liquid. "I was wrong," he said. "We didn't need the amulet. We needed her blood. That's what held the greatest magic."

Meaghan shook her head. "But, she turned to ashes. We don't have her blood."

"Monty was her son," he reminded her.

He emptied the vial into the bowl, and suddenly, purple smoke rose into the air. Fitz carefully mixed the potion as it boiled and steamed, bubbling up to the edge of the bowl. Then, when it stopped boiling, he dipped his finger into the mixture.

"Tristan," he said, "you should be first."

Tristan came forward, his hair now completely gray and his face lined with wrinkles. Fitz put his finger on Tristan's forehead and applied the potion across his temple. Suddenly, the lines on his face filled out, his hair darkened, and he stood taller.

"It seems the spell is broken," he said, but there was little joy in his voice.

Turning, Tristan took Meaghan's hands and pulled her away from the table. He cradled her chin in his hand and gently wiped away the tracks of her tears. "I am so sorry for all the pain you have had to bear for us," he whispered.

She shook her head. "No, this is not your fault," she said. "It's just..." Her voice broke and filled with sorrow. "It's just what was meant to be."

He pulled her into his arms and held her. "Come back with me," he whispered urgently. "Come back to Camelot with me."

She leaned back and looked at him and saw the love in his eyes. "You..." she paused.

He smiled down at her. "I love you with all my heart," he answered her unspoken question. "I cannot survive without you. Come back with me. Come back and be my wife."

Joy filled all the places sorrow had left empty. She smiled at him, her heart in her eyes, and nodded. "Yes," she said. "Yes, I will come back with you. I have nothing left for me here."

He leaned down to claim her lips.

"Tristan," Fitz exclaimed. "We must go now. The sun is in position."

Tristan smiled at her. "You owe me a kiss," he whispered and then took her hand and led her back to the group. "I have the best news. Meaghan is coming back with us, and she will become my wife."

"Well, that's the wisest decision you've ever made," Rufus said, patting Tristan on the back.

"Congratulations," Garrett added. "I've never met a finer lady than you, Lady Meaghan. I'm happy for you, Tristan."

"Thank you, Sir Garrett," Meaghan replied. "I'm so—"

"That will be impossible," Fitz said sadly.

"What?" Tristan asked. "Why? She has nothing left here. Her family, her friends are all gone. We cannot leave her here!"

"If she comes back with us, it will change history. She will no longer be in her time, but in ours," Fitz said. "And if she changes history, there is a great chance that Morganna will go free."

"But there's also a chance that everything will be fine," Tristan argued. "We don't know with any certainty that it will change anything at all."

Fitz turned to Meaghan. "Are you willing to take that chance?" he asked.

Chapter Fifty-seven

Meaghan glanced over at Monty's body lying still and cold on the ground, and she pulled her hand from Tristan's grasp. She took a step back and shook her head. "No," she whispered, her voice filled with pain. "No, I cannot take that chance. Would you stay here with the chance that she would be free?"

He paused and then closed his eyes, shaking his head. "No, I would not," he confessed. "But, Meaghan, I love you."

"And I love you," she replied. "But I suppose sometimes that's just not enough."

"It has to be enough," Tristan argued. "Meaghan, you've sacrificed enough."

She shook her head and turned to Fitz. "What would you have me do?"

He placed his hand on her shoulder and met her eyes. She could see the love and concern in them. "Go back to your home," he said. "And live the kind of life you were always meant to live."

She shook her head. "I'm afraid that is impossible," she replied.

He smiled gently. "Dear Lady Meaghan, the world is filled with possibilities."

He lifted his hand from her shoulder and turned to the knights. "Gather together, each of you placing a hand on the shoulder of the man next to you," he ordered, tucking the bowl with the potion into his arm.

Meaghan watched as the men created a circle in the middle of the ruin. She could see the frustration and disappointment in Tristan's eyes, and she prayed that someday he would find it in his heart to forgive her. She listened to Fitz recite the words of the time spell and watched as they slowly disappeared from view.

"I will always love you," she whispered, tears coursing from her eyes. Then she looked around the ruin and saw the remnants of her life all around her— Monty's body, Jepson's spear, Fitz's saddlebag, and her sword. There was nothing left. Tristan's voice echoed in her mind. *She has nothing left here. Her family, her friends are all gone.*

He was right. She had nothing. She had no one.

Suddenly, the pain was too much. She dropped to her knees and buried her face in her hands, allowing the grief to pour out of her soul through her tears. Finally, exhausted, she lay down on the ground and slept.

***

She awoke with a start. It was night, and the moon shone brightly in the sky above her. She heard a noise and reached for her sword, but she couldn't find it.

"Don't worry. Your sword is where you left it."

Meaghan looked in the direction of the voice. The little man she had encountered twice was standing several feet away from her. Her voice was rough and raspy when she used it. "I beg your pardon," she said, sitting up. "I would not have used the sword on you."

He smiled at her. "I do not blame you for waking ready to fight, milady," he replied. "Your life, these past weeks, has not been easy."

She took a deep breath and nodded. "I will agree with you, good sir," she acknowledged.

Turning, she looked over her shoulder and gasped, then quickly turned back to him. "Monty's body," she said. "My friend. My friend's body was there," she exclaimed, scrambling to her feet. "Do you know where it is? Has someone taken it?"

"Time has always been a difficult concept for mortals, has it not?" he asked.

She shook her head. "I don't understand."

"While you slept, time changed," he replied. "Merlin and the knights returned to Camelot. A new future was created."

She still just stared at him, befuddled. "What?"

"If Morganna never came into the future, Monty was never born," he explained. "And if he wasn't born, he did not die."

"They made it back then?" she asked, a glimmer of hope filling her.

He nodded and smiled. "Yes, milady. They made it back," he replied. "And now it is time for you to journey back to your own life."

"It will not be much of a life," she confessed. "But I am determined to see it through." She walked across the room, picked up her sword and held it out to him. "This is really yours, but I thank you for the loan."

He shook his head. "Oh no, milady," he said. "You have made it your own. It belongs to you now."

She placed it in the scabbard and nodded. "Thank you," she said. "To tell the truth, I was loath to leave it. There is no telling what I will encounter on my journey home."

"Ah, and that, milady, is why I am here," he said. "To offer you a map that will take you through the areas of the fae where we will protect you and shorten your journey's time."

He held out a piece of old parchment to her. She unrolled it and saw that it went through the mountains. "But how…"

"There are places in this world, thin places, that mortals can sense but do not understand," he said. "These places are portals and can hasten your journey home. We fae are in debt to you. The balance of good and evil has been restored, thanks to your efforts. We will not forget it."

Chapter Fifty-eight

Tristan was amazed that the journey that had taken him and his companions a thousand years to travel was reversed in just a few moments. The men looked around the room. A castle now stood where the ruins had stood just minutes ago.

"Can it be true?" Rufus asked, his voice thick with emotion. "Are we truly home?"

"Yes," Fitz said. "And if we want to keep it this way, we can waste no time confronting Morganna."

He started to walk towards the door when Tristan stopped him. "Hold for a moment, Merlin," he said. "If we arrive in Camelot after she has set the spell in place, does she still not have the advantage? Can we not use this same spell to go back and capture her before she obtains it?"

Fitz smiled slowly. "An excellent plan," he said, nodding in agreement. "Shall we lay a trap for the Lady Sorceress?"

*   *   *

Morganna's black carriage sped along the beach toward her castle on the Isle of Avalon. She had used much of her fortune to pay those who had connection with the Dark Arts for information that would eventually help her to destroy King Arthur completely. She sat back in the comfort of her carriage, stroking her amulet fondly as she thought of the ramifications of a spell that could move a person in time.

"A simple dagger through Igraine's womb would quickly solve the problem," she mused, speaking of King Arthur's mother. "Then Arthur would have never been born."

She glanced out the window to see her castle coming into view. "Hurry," she called to her driver. "We must be finished before high tide."

The driver whipped the horses on, and the carriage sped through the sand and up the road to the castle. Morganna barely waited for the carriage to stop before she alighted and hurried toward the entrance. Her footmen hurried after her, but she turned and waved them off. "I have private business," she snapped. "Wait for me at the carriage."

She entered the Great Hall and saw a man, dressed in a dark cloak, waiting for her.

"Well met, sir," she said as she walked to him. "Have you the document?"

The man nodded his head, his face concealed by the cloak. "Have you the money?" he replied.

She smiled. "No honor among thieves," she retorted. "Do you believe that I, a lone woman, would bring such an amount in without verification of the document?"

"I have heard of your power, milady," the man replied. "And I am not convinced that once I relinquish my document that you will not turn me into a rodent for the wolves to devour."

She laughed and nodded. "That does sound like something I would do," she countered. "And so, it seems, we are at an impasse."

"Not an impasse," the man said. "But perhaps a handshake, to bind our agreement."

Morganna decided the man was a fool if he thought a mere handshake would keep her from killing him and taking both the document and the money. "Of course. What an excellent solution, sir," she said, extending her hand.

He enclosed her hand in his own and then wiped his finger against her wrist. She immediately began to feel her skin burn.

"What is this?" she exclaimed, pulling her hand away and examining the smudge of purple on her wrist.

Merlin pushed back the hood and felt a great deal of satisfaction when she gasped in shock. "It is only a binding spell, Lady Morganna," he said. "Relinquishing you of all your power."

She could feel herself weaken, feel her strength drain from her being. "No," she gasped. "This cannot be. No binding spell can be created…"

"Without the use of the participant's blood," Merlin finished for her. "Which is why it is very wise to not venture into the future where all manner of things can be found."

She shook her head. "You won't get away with this," she cried. "My men…"

"Are now under the watchful eyes of some of King Arthur's knights," he finished, "who will also be very happy to escort you back to Camelot where you will spend the rest of your days imprisoned in the tower."

"No, this can't be happening," she screamed.

Merlin shrugged. "Oh, but it is."

Chapter Fifty-nine

Dawn was breaking when Meaghan rode out of the forest near her own home. The dew sat heavy on the grass, and the scent of lilacs floated in the morning breeze. She kept her gaze pointedly fixed on the hills alongside the woods because she wasn't ready to once again see the burnt remains of her home. She was grateful that the acrid smell of the fire no longer lay heavy in the air.

She'd done a lot of thinking during her ride through the faery forest and had decided that she would initially seek refuge in the gypsy camp until she decided what she wanted to do with her life.

She turned her horse from the road into the high grass of the pasture toward the hills that housed the camp.

"I thought I would find you here."

Meaghan gasped in horror at the specter that stood before her.

"What's wrong with you, Lady Meaghan?" Daisy asked. "You look like you've just seen a ghost."

Meaghan slid off her horse and walked slowly toward her old friend, shaking her head in terrified wonder. "Daisy, is it really you?" she stammered, tears filling her eyes. "You're alive."

"It's me, the same way it was me this morning when you left for your ride," Daisy said, shocked when Meaghan hugged her. "Did you hit your head or something when you were out in those woods?" Then her eyes widened, and she stepped back. "Or did the fae do something to your mind? Have they taken away your good sense?"

Meaghan dropped her arms, smiled and wiped away her tears. "How long have I been away?" she asked.

Daisy shrugged. "A little over an hour," she replied. "Did something happen while you were gone?"

"It has been an unusual ride," she said. "And I dare say I am not my usual self this morning."

"Well, and it can be expected with all the excitement," Daisy replied. "Now hurry on. You need to get dressed before the company arrives."

"Company?" Meaghan asked, walking alongside Daisy in the meadow.

They had just crested the small hill in the meadow, and Meaghan froze in her tracks. There laying before her, in its pristine beauty, was the manor house, it's pink stone glowing in the early morning sun.

"They're not dead," she whispered, tears flowing down her face. She turned to Daisy, smiling through her tears. "They're not dead!"

She broke into a run, speeding down the hill at a breakneck pace and skidding slightly sideways when she jumped from meadow onto the graveled walkways of the garden. She quickly recovered her footing and dashed up the garden steps, past several amused gardeners, and sprinted to the front door. She pushed the door open. Gasping and crying, she threw herself into the arms of her parents, who were standing at the foot of the stairs.

"Meggie? What's wrong?" her father asked, holding his sobbing daughter in his arms. "Did something happen to you?"

"Meaghan, darling, please say something," her mother pleaded.

Meaghan looked up at her parents, their features blurry behind the veil of her tears, and shook her head. "I just..." she began, her body shaking and her voice trembling. "I just love you both so much."

"We love you, too," her mother replied, hugging her daughter and sending a look of concern over her head to her husband. "Why don't you just go upstairs and rest for a bit?"

Meaghan nodded. "I will," she agreed. "I will in just a moment."

They had done it! They had stopped Morganna and changed everything. But she had to be sure. "Father, what is the Herdin family motto?" she asked.

Her father looked confused and shook his head. "I'm not sure I know," he said. "Something about heart, I believe. Why?"

She grinned. "No reason," she said. "No reason at all. And Fitz…is Fitz…" Then she stopped and shook her head. "Well, no, of course not. Fitz wouldn't be here."

"Darling, who is this Fitz person?" her mother asked.

"An old friend," she said with a smile. "A very old friend."

She heard the crunching of horse hooves on gravel and turned to see Daisy leading her horse toward the stables. "Here you are, Jepson," she heard Daisy say. "Lady Meaghan's horse."

Meaghan turned and ran out of the house. "Jepson!" she shouted, running down the steps toward him. "Jepson, you're alive!"

She threw herself into his arms, and he held her for a long moment. "Thank you," he whispered. "You broke the spell."

She looked up. "You remember?" she asked quietly.

He nodded. "Every moment," he said. "But no one else does. It will be our secret."

"Did people think you were crazy when you came back?" she asked.

He smiled at her. "I believe I was a little quieter about my surprise," he said.

She laughed, and it felt wonderful to do it. "I suppose I should tell them I bumped my head," she said quietly.

He nodded. "Before they call the doctor."

"That's good advice," she agreed with a smile.

"Oh, one more thing," he whispered.

"Yes?"

"Tonight is your coming out party," he said. "People from all over the area have been invited."

"But I just got back," she replied, dismayed.

"Not in this reality," he said. "So, I'm afraid you still have one more burden to bear."

She sighed and nodded. "Thank you," she said. "One more burden indeed."

Chapter Sixty

Tristan sat alone in a booth in the corner of the pub, nursing a pint of ale and staring morosely at the wooden panels across from him. His face held several days' worth of stubble. His clothing was dirty, and his hair was unkempt.

"My, don't we present a picture of honor and knighthood," Sir Garrett commented as he slid in the booth across from Tristan.

"Go away," Tristan growled sullenly.

Garrett sat back and grinned. "I wondered if it was merely infatuation, or the excitement of the adventure, or true love," he commented easily. Then he sniffed the air and twisted his face in disgust. "And by the look and smell of things, I would venture to say it was true love."

Tristan glanced up at him. "It was true love, damn you," he said. "And now, if you're done, you can be on your way."

Garrett stretched out his legs and crossed them casually. "And I would suppose that Lady

Meaghan would be home by now," he said. "Enjoying the benefits of home and hearth."

He looked down at his fingernails and shrugged. "Who knows? But I would venture to say that all the eligible suitors for miles around would be pounding on the door."

"Do you want to wear this pint, Garrett?"

Garrett chuckled softly. "Oh, by the way, Rufus and his family are doing very well," he said. "Of course, they had no idea they were separated for so long, but Rufus has not let any of them out of sight since he's been home."

"That's good to know," Tristan replied, his tone more controlled.

"I wonder," Garrett mused. "Did you ever wonder about the children you and Lady Meaghan would have had?"

"Enough," Tristan growled.

"At least one boy," Garrett continued, "so Meaghan could teach him how to use a sword. And a little girl to wrap her father around her tiny finger, following her mother's example."

Tristan didn't respond this time, just closed his eyes and placed his forehead in his hands.

"Oh, I don't think you've heard," Garrett continued. "Our own Andrew is engaged to that…bar wench. I forget her name…"

"Anwyn," Tristan growled.

Garrett snapped his fingers. "Right you are. Anwyn. Seeing that we stopped Morganna before she got the spell, the girl is no longer dead. Which makes for a much more desirable courtship."

Tristan sighed. "Is there a point to this torment?"

Garrett shrugged. "Why yes, now that you ask, there is. But I have not finished yet."

Tristan sat back against the booth and glared at Garrett. "Please, continue."

Nodding politely, Garrett grinned. "Duncan has also found himself a love interest."

Tristan's raised eyebrow was his only response.

"Yes, I found that unbelievable myself," Garrett said. "The scholar said that the example of

Lady Meaghan caused him to rethink his relationship with the weaker sex. He even went so far as to postulate they might not be the weaker sex after all."

Tristan sighed heavily.

"Ah, I am so glad you asked me about myself," Garrett continued. "I hate to admit, but your Lady Meaghan taught me a lot about love and sacrifice." His voice softened. "And what's truly worth fighting about and for. I am happy to report that my sister and I have been reconciled, and she is to be married."

Tristan felt the sting of tears in his eyes. "I am happy for you," he whispered. "I truly am."

Garrett smiled at his friend. "Thank you," he said. "And now, I will leave you."

He stood up and started to walk away from the booth. But then he turned and placing both hands on the table leaned forward so he was nearly in Tristan's face. "But if I knew a wizard who owed me a favor and who had a spell that could send me forward in time," he said pointedly, "I sure as hell wouldn't be drinking my life away in a pub."

He pushed himself away from the table and watched with a satisfied smile as his words sunk in.

Tristan slid out of the booth and started to run past him, but Garrett grabbed him by his collar. "Make sure you clean yourself before you go," he teased. "Even true love has its limits."

Chapter Sixty-one

Meaghan stared at herself in the looking glass with a bittersweet mix of emotions. She was dressed as a princess; her gown was the most beautiful combination of nearly sheer organza layered over a silk underdress she had ever seen. She would most certainly be a success, as her parents had been repeating all day. And truly, for their sake, she wanted to be a success. She wanted to do everything in her power to make them happy. But, she wondered as she stepped forward and looked closer at her reflection, would they be able to discern the sadness in her eyes? Would they know that she would never make a brilliant match because she could never pretend to love another?

"Lady Meaghan," Daisy said from the doorway, "it's time."

Taking one last look at herself in the mirror, Meaghan turned and smiled at Daisy. "Thank you," she said. "I'm ready."

They walked down the hall together toward the sweeping staircase. "Lord Monty is to lead you down," Daisy said.

"Monty's here?" Meaghan breathed. "But how…"

"His parents' estate is only a few miles to the east," Daisy said. "Besides, your parents thought that Monty would be the best choice because you've been friends for so long."

A terrible thought entered Meaghan's mind, and she put her hand on Daisy's arm to stop her. "Monty and I, we're just friends, nothing else?" she asked.

Daisy smiled at her. "You two couldn't be more brother and sister if you were born to the same parents," she said. "You don't have to worry about Monty sniffing after your skirts."

Breathing a sigh of relief, Meaghan nodded. "Okay, let's go."

Daisy walked with Meaghan to the top of the stairs. "Wait here," she said. "I'll go get Monty."

Daisy turned and slipped through the door to the servant's staircase. Meaghan glanced at the door, the one she used daily to sneak up to her room and change from her riding gear, and wondered if she could use the same staircase to escape her coming out party.

"You've faced Morganna with a sword," she chided herself. "Surely you can face a room full of suitors."

"I beg your pardon? Did you say something, Meggie?" her mother asked.

Meaghan shook her head. "I'm sorry, mother. I'm just muttering to myself," she replied.

Her mother stood back and looked at her daughter, then hugged her. "You look beautiful," she said. "As I knew you would." Then her face dropped a little, and a look of aggravation crossed it.

"What's wrong?" Meaghan asked.

With an exasperated sigh, her mother took Meaghan's hand and pulled her away from the staircase. "We've just received a note that Monty and his parents will be arriving a little late," she said, trying to keep the anger from her voice. "It seems that Lady Strathmore's preparations for the night are taking longer than she planned. One would think that my daughter's needs would take precedence over Lady Strathmore's need to paint her face." She took a deep breath and smiled. "But, what is done is done."

Meaghan shrugged. "I can just come down the stairs on my own," she suggested.

"Oh no, dear," her mother replied. "That is simply not done." She smiled again. "However, it seems that we have a baronet visiting from just outside our district. He has spoken with your father and would be more than happy to escort you."

"A stranger?' Meaghan asked, her stomach knotting.

Her mother nodded. "And so I told your father," she agreed. "So, we arranged for you to meet him in the library before he escorts you downstairs. He is waiting for you as we speak."

Meaghan took a deep breath and smiled. "Well, then, I suppose I should go introduce myself to my escort."

The library was situated on the second floor in her parents' wing. It was a large room, with tall, floor to ceiling shelves filled with books. Dark velvet curtains ran down the outside wall, covering the windows, and a fireplace was banked for the evening and glowing softly. Meaghan loved this room. It had so many good memories of family time with her parents. She entered the room, closed the door behind her and noted that her escort was across the room standing in the shadows.

She curtsied politely. "Good evening, sir," she said. "I thank you for stepping in at the last moment."

He nodded. "The pleasure is all mine," he replied. "But, if I may be so bold, may I ask why I have been given this honor?"

She smiled. "That is a fair question," she replied, straining to see his hidden face. "It would seem that my former escort's mother is still making preparations for her entrance, and so they are all delayed."

"If my betrothed were awaiting me, I would not allow my mother to hinder my arrival."

Meaghan laughed. "Monty is not my betrothed. We are as brother and sister in our relationship."

"And there are no other men who hold claim to your heart?"

She sighed and felt tears in the back of her eyes. "There is but one," she replied. "And, so you understand from the onset, although this is my coming out, I do not plan to marry."

"So, you do not believe in love?" he asked.

She gasped softly; the pain was so real. "Oh, sir, you misjudge me," she said quietly. "I believe in love. But I also believe that you give your heart but once, and mine is already spoken for."

The man was silent for a long moment, and then he asked. "Do you believe in magic?"

"I don't understand," she replied, shaking her head.

He stepped forward into the light.

"Tristan?" she breathed, her body trembling with joy. "Is it really you?"

He rushed forward and caught her in his arms, then lowered his lips and claimed hers. He showered her face with kisses and then returned to her lips to capture her soft moans. "I have waited for nearly an eternity for you," he whispered against her lips. "Say you'll marry me. Say you'll be mine forever."

"Yes," she cried happily. "Yes, my heart has always been yours."

He crushed her lips with his, and time stood still for both of them.

The End

About the author: Terri Reid lives near Freeport, the home of the Mary O'Reilly Mystery Series, and loves a good ghost story. An independent author, Reid uploaded her first book "Loose Ends – A Mary O'Reilly Paranormal Mystery" in August 2010. By the end of 2013, "Loose Ends" had sold over 200,000 copies. She has sixteen other books in the Mary O'Reilly Series, the first books in the following series - "The Blackwood Files," "The Order of Brigid's Cross," and "The Legend of the Horsemen." She also has a stand-alone romance, "Bearly in Love." Reid has enjoyed Top Rated and Hot New Release status in the Women Sleuths and Paranormal Romance category through Amazon US. Her books have been translated into Spanish, Portuguese and German and are also now also available in print and audio versions. Reid has been quoted in several books about the self-publishing industry including "Let's Get Digital" by David Gaughran and "Interviews with Indie Authors: Top Tips from Successful Self-Published Authors" by Claire and Tim Ridgway. She was also honored to have some of her works included in A. J. Abbiati's book "The NORTAV Method for Writers – The Secrets to Constructing Prose Like the Pros."

She loves hearing from her readers at author@terrireid.com

Other Books by Terri Reid:

Mary O'Reilly Paranormal Mystery Series:

Mary O'Reilly Short Stories

Tales Around the Jack O'Lantern 3

Auld Lang Syne

The Order of Brigid's Cross (Sean's Story)

The Wild Hunt (Book 1)

The Faery Portal (Book 2)

The Blackwood Files (Art's Story)

File One: Family Secrets

File Two: Private Wars

PRCD Case Files: The Ghosts Of New Orleans -A Paranormal Research and Containment Division Case File

Eochaidh: Legend of the Horseman (Book One)

Sweet Romances

Bearly in Love

Sneakers – A Swift Romance

Lethal Distraction – A Pierogies & Pumps Mystery Novella

Made in the USA
Lexington, KY
12 September 2018